I0622044

BEAUTIFULLY BLUE

CANDIED CRUSH #7

CHARITY PARKERSON

The scanning, uploading, and distributing of this book via the internet or via any other means without the permission of the copyright owner is illegal and punishable by law. Criminal copyright infringement, including infringement without monetary gain, is investigated by the FBI and is punishable by up to 5 years in federal prison and a fine of $250,000. Please purchase only authorized electronic editions and do not participate in or encourage electronic piracy of copyrighted materials. Brief passages may be quoted for review purposes if credit is given to the copyright holder. Your support of the author's rights is appreciated. Any resemblances to person(s) living or dead, is completely coincidental. All items contained within this novel are products of the author's imagination.

—Warning: This book is intended for readers over the age of 18.

Copyright © 2020 Charity Parkerson
Editor: BZ Hercules & Consultants
Photographer: Pick Your Pic
ISBN: 978-1-946099-77-8
All rights reserved.

❀ Created with Vellum

INTRODUCTION

A WELL-KNOWN ACTOR MEETS AN EVERYDAY
COP. WHAT COULD GO WRONG? EVERYTHING.

When Valor met his celebrity crush, Reid King, he never expected Reid would show any interest in him. While Valor isn't lacking in confidence, Reid is considerably younger than him and could have anyone. It makes no sense for a man like Reid to want a middle-aged cop. Unless he needs someone to save him.

In reality, Reid is everything one would expect a star to be. He's arrogant, self-absorbed, and used to having his way. When he met Valor, Reid knew he could have the man with little to no effort. He wasn't wrong. Reid just didn't expect he would need Valor as much as he does.

With Reid's past exposed for public fodder, Reid is struggling with a new sense of self. As much as he wants to be with Valor, he questions his every life decision now and can't stop ruining everything. He worries he won't ever be whole again. All he needs is a man in blue to rescue him. If Reid will let him, that is. It's also possible he's not the only one who needs saving.

AUTHOR NOTE

This book has triggers. Nothing on page. Just two people trying to survive adulthood while dealing with traumatic pasts.

ONE

AS PER USUAL for a Saturday night, Valor was alone. There weren't a lot of guys on the force willing to take in a play with Valor after work, so Valor saw most shows alone. Valor didn't mind hitting The Coastal Arts Center by himself. The place was vast and interesting. Plus, once everyone found their seats, it didn't matter that he didn't have anyone at his side. He couldn't see anything besides the stage. Valor disappeared inside the story. Tonight, he had sprung for a seat as close to the front as he could get. Usually, Valor chose the cheapest seats. This show was different because Reid King played the lead.

Eight months ago, Valor had met Reid at an art

gallery while visiting a friend. Well, Dawson was more like a son than a friend and the art gallery belonged to Dawson's husband, Milo. Semantics. The outcome had been the same. Valor had met the onetime Hollywood actor turned stage performer while visiting Dawson. Reid and he had immediately clicked. While Valor had been an enormous fan of Reid's before they met, that had little to do with his immediate attraction. They genuinely had more in common than Valor had found with anyone in a long time. He had taken Reid to dinner that night, and they had spent the entire night trying to talk over each other. They had been so wrapped up in telling each other stories that they had ended up back at Reid's place, where they had talked until the sun came up before falling asleep on opposite ends of the couch. They hadn't kissed until their fourth date. Neither of them shut up long enough to kiss until Reid had finally pressed his lips to Valor's mid-sentence. It was the first time Valor felt more than lust for anyone. Not that he didn't want Reid. Valor did. Having Reid's sexy body beneath him occupied Valor's mind way more than he cared to admit, especially since things had gone to hell swiftly afterward.

Like most things that were too good to be true, Reid's attention had turned out to be fake. Reid had met Valor as a complete fluke while being blackmailed by an ex co-star and trying to break up Dawson's marriage. Everything between Reid and Valor changed upon that admission, except for how Valor felt. That was why he kept coming to these shows. That, and the way Reid's powerful presence seemed to shake the walls of the playhouse with each performance.

Valor leaned forward in his seat as Reid's voice rose and fell, keeping perfect time with the musical. He was born for this. Valor was captivated. Acting—like anything else—was just a job, but it took something special. Not just anyone could take the stage and win an audience, carrying an entire production to success. Reid could do that. It was powerful to behold. Valor felt like he sat in the presence of greatness and he was moved by it. It really was no wonder that Valor meant nothing to someone like Reid. Still, for a moment, Valor had held the world.

By the time the cast took their bows, Valor had a catch in his throat. Nothing got to him quite like the stage. As long as Valor could recall, he had been a huge follower. But tonight, it was all for Reid. In fact, he swore—for a moment—their gazes met and held. Valor never missed anyone once they were gone. He missed Reid now that the man wanted nothing to do with him any longer. It was all Valor's fault.

THE RACING IN REID'S CHEST WAS HALF adrenaline and half longing. Doing live shows never got old. He loved the theater. Off stage, things were different. Harder. Acting came easy for Reid. After all, he had been pretending happiness his entire life. Smiling on stage was nothing. Tonight, his smile had been real. The moment he stepped on stage, Reid had spotted him. Valor had been right up front. His gaze had never wavered from Reid. Reid knew because he had felt Valor's intensity like a physical touch. Now that the show was over, Reid only had the memories again, and the catty stares of his co-stars.

Everything about his life was different now. This time last year, Reid had been on top. While he still got all the starring roles he could handle, people treated him differently now. Reid wanted to say that was on Valor, but it wasn't. Not really. Reid made his bed well over a decade ago, and now everyone knew it.

"Some guy passed this along."

Reid didn't reach for the scrap of paper right away. An overwhelming sense of dread rose inside Reid as he stared at the stagehand. Nowadays, he never knew what he would get from strangers. His breath came out sounding shaky as he thanked the guy and accepted. Reid waited until he was alone before glancing at the business card in his hand. It was some kind of car wash. Reid flipped it over. A smile snapped to his lips as he read.

Sorry about the card. It was all I had. I'm headed to The Back Porch. If you'd like to meet, I'll be there. If not, I understand. I know you're busy—Valor.

Reid wasn't sure how he felt. About eight months ago, when he first met Valor, Reid had never been more interested in anyone. He couldn't explain it. They just clicked. Valor turned Reid into a chatterbox. With Valor, Reid felt comfortable in his own skin and safe. Unfortunately, that instant connection had come with a single harsh reality. The only way they could be together was if Reid came clean about why they had met in the first place. They had met in an art gallery. Reid had been there to purposely destroy someone's marriage. That person was someone Valor considered a son. Reid could make all the excuses if he wanted to do so. He had been blackmailed, after all. He would like to think he wasn't capable of destroying someone's marriage otherwise. The thing was, though, someone had been able to blackmail Reid for a reason. He was an awful person.

Reid held tight to Valor's card and stared at his reflection in the mirror. He liked to think he had earned this dressing room through hard work. Maybe he had. Reid had also traded his soul, or rather, his mother had. That depended upon who someone asked. His therapist said Reid wasn't at fault. After all, he had been a child when he sucked his first dick for stardom. Reid's throat swelled. Sometimes, he felt like a victim. Whenever he thought back on those days, he immediately felt sick to his stomach and robbed of his youth. Most of the time, though, Reid felt nothing at all. This life had made him hard. Cold. He didn't recall being unwilling at the time, even though he understood now that he hadn't been old enough to make those decisions. Reid had been a child used by adults, but still. He had reaped the rewards. This career had started on a foundation of ugliness. It was harder than Reid had ever anticipated, having people know the truth.

Valor had done that. He had saved Reid from a blackmailer by exposing everything. Reid still hadn't decided if he had been rescued or ruined. It felt a lot like both. Still, coffee at The Back Porch seemed harmless enough. Reid had always liked the popular coffeehouse. It was a quiet place for people who didn't like to party but enjoyed meeting likeminded people. In this case, other gay men. It was a nice spot. Reid had never been there before Valor had taken him. Maybe a harmless coffee would ease the pains in Reid's chest when he thought about Valor. It certainly couldn't make anything worse.

AT ONLY AN HOUR UNTIL THE BACK PORCH closed, Valor wondered if he should just go home. Reid obviously didn't intend to meet him. The nearly empty coffee house resembled Valor's life more than he liked to admit. Even though being a policeman had always been Valor's calling, he didn't truly fit in. He worked alone and went home to an empty house. For four years, he had been blessed to have his friend Dawson living in his detached garage. That had given his life a bit of sound. Since Dawson had gotten married and moved to Santa Barbara,

Valor's life had been pretty quiet. He tried not to look at things too closely. At forty, Valor recognized he might have passed the age of anyone wanting to settle down with him. Valor didn't know if he even wanted that. Things were quiet, though.

Valor sipped his drink. He would stay until closing time. After all, he had nothing to go home to but silence. A few people still lingered in a curved booth, talking and laughing. The noise made Valor feel less alone. Still, when the door swung open, Valor's head shot up and hope filled his chest. A subdued-looking Reid stepped inside. His blue gaze scanned the room before landing on Valor. He didn't smile. Valor's heart skipped a beat nonetheless. Reid was gorgeous. His dark, unkempt hair brushed his collar. His full lips caught and held Valor's attention. The guy looked like a star and he had shown up. Valor fought the urge to stand and greet him, since he didn't want to appear too enthusiastic.

Reid pulled out a chair across from Valor and sat.

"I didn't think you would show." Valor couldn't stop the words from bursting from him.

"Then why did you wait?"

Valor shrugged. "I'm an optimist, I suppose." Valor tried to smile, but it slipped. "You've been avoiding me."

Reid rearranged the sugar shaker and the menus while not meeting Valor's stare. "Not avoiding, really. I've been busy. A lot of work goes into getting ready for a big production." Reid stopped fidgeting and finally met Valor's stare. "Plus, you did put all my business out in public. Obviously, I realize it had to be done and you saved me from a blackmailer, but I also lost a few roles over the scandal. No one wants to work with someone controversial." Reid's gaze slid away again. He scratched the side of his nose. "But it's not like I hate you or anything."

Valor didn't know how to respond to that one, because he wasn't so sure Reid spoke the truth. He chose to move on. "It's good to see you. You were amazing tonight."

Reid went back to moving the bottles and sugar packets caddy, as if arranging everything by height. "I'm glad you enjoyed the show."

Without thought, Valor covered Reid's hand, stopping him from rearranging the contents of the table again. "Why are you so nervous with me?"

Reid's gaze snapped to Valor's and didn't move. "Why did you want to see me?"

A smile stretched Valor's lips. He didn't need to think about it. "I always want to see you, but—like I said—you've been avoiding me."

Reid shook his head. A small smile played on his lips. "Isn't this place about to close? Who drinks coffee this late at night? Isn't it closer to wine o'clock?"

Valor bit his bottom lip, trying not to smile like an idiot. "Are you trying to lure me to a second location?"

The humor disappeared from Reid's expression. "I'm sorry. I didn't mean to make you feel that way." Reid stood and shoved his hands in his pockets. "It was good to see you."

Valor's forehead furrowed. He didn't understand what he had done wrong. Confusion slowed him. Reid was already headed for the door before Valor rushed to follow. He waited until they were outside before picking up speed and calling out. "Hold up. Reid. Wait. I haven't seen you in forever. Can I just have like five minutes?"

Reid leaned against the door of his dark blue BMW and waited for Valor to catch up. He chewed the side of his thumbnail, looking like he didn't know what to do with his hands.

Valor came to stand toe to toe with him. He gently tugged Reid's hand away from his face. Valor hated that Reid looked so lost, especially when he still looked so goddamn confident on stage only hours earlier. "Tell me what I did wrong?"

Reid didn't try pulling away. He let Valor keep a hold on his hand. His throat moved, as if he swallowed past a painful lump. "I'm sorry. This is why I haven't called. I don't know how to act around you anymore. You're the guy who knows too much."

"What do I know?" Valor took a step closer and answered his own question before Reid could. "I know that you're amazing and I thought we had a spark. If you're saying that I know you blow me away, you're right. You're the greatest guy I've met in a long time. I don't think I can be blamed for wishing you would keep coming around, but I get it if you can't." Valor kissed Reid's hand before letting it slip away. "Thank you for letting me dream for five minutes."

Valor headed for his truck without looking back. Even though Valor knew it had been a long shot that someone like Reid King could possibly care about him, he could live with knowing he had tried. After all, only a fool would have passed up the chance. Tomorrow, he might not feel so bad about how things had gone. When the sun came up, Valor would remind himself that he had done a good thing, saving a lot of people by exposing

Reid's blackmailer, and in turn putting a serial pedophile behind bars. Tonight, though, Valor felt like shit. He genuinely cared about Reid and wanted to keep pursuing what they had started eight months ago. Valor knew a lost cause when he saw one. Reid was done with him. There was nothing Valor could do to save them.

TWO

AFTER SPENDING MOST of the night awake, thinking about how fucked up he was, Reid made one solid decision. He liked Valor. That was why he currently stood on Valor's doorstep with fresh croissants and coffee at eight in the morning. It didn't occur to him that Valor might not be off work today until his third time of ringing the doorbell went unanswered. The place was a small three-bedroom brick home. Reid imagined the doorbell wouldn't be hard to hear. Valor's truck was in the driveway, but that didn't mean anything.

A patrol car turned in to the driveway. Reid eyed the car. Valor was behind the wheel. He parked close to the sidewalk leading to the front door and stepped out.

As Reid headed his way, Valor motioned toward the house. "I saw you on the doorbell camera and I was close by."

Reid turned bashful, which he fucking hated. Before Valor had learned all his secrets, Reid had been bold and confident in the man's presence. Now he was just a mess. He fell back on the one thing that never failed him—acting. Reid pasted on a bright smile. He nodded toward the boxes he held. "I brought you breakfast. Croissants and coffee. There are some fresh strawberry preserves as well."

For a moment, Valor didn't look interested in anything Reid had to offer.

Oddly, that bolstered Reid's confidence. Reid's smile turned genuine. "Would you be more tempted if I said I made them? I didn't, but we could pretend."

Valor smiled. It wasn't an enormous grin or anything, but he looked a hair more welcoming. He pointed toward the passenger side of his patrol car. "Get in."

With a sharp nod, Reid moved to do as told.

Valor slid behind the wheel. "I'm still on duty, but there's nothing stopping us from going for a ride."

Reid put on his seatbelt. "Sounds good. You

drive and I'll feed you." Reid bit his lip and dropped his gaze to the boxes in his lap. Valor's expression had happiness growing in his chest. The way Valor visibly fought a smile made Reid proud—like maybe he wasn't failing completely at everything outside his career. Reid had never been the greatest at reality. That was why he loved the theater. He got to pretend to be someone else. Reid wasn't very good at being just Reid.

He pulled a coffee from the cardboard container and set it in Valor's cup holder. "Two creams and four sugars. The way you like it." Reid flipped open the lid on the box. "These are honey butter croissants. They're really good with the strawberry stuff, but I recommend trying a bite without it, in case it's too sweet for you." Flakes went everywhere as Reid pulled apart one of the rolls and popped it into Valor's open and waiting mouth. He brushed the crumbs from his fingers before swiping at Valor's uniform.

"Damn. That's good. Where did you find these?"

"Not easily," Reid admitted. "There's this guy who brings them in for the cast. He's the best pastry chef I have ever met, but he doesn't have an actual shop. More or less, he just has side deals with a few businesses around town. Like, the theater pays him to drop off a variety of things and a few eclectic shops let him sell his creations there. I had to drive around a bit looking for them this morning. In the end, I called Tobin and got them directly from him."

"You should put him in touch with Wrecker. These would be great at his shop. Slather some of that strawberry on there. I want to try that."

Reid took bites between feeding Valor. Even though they were in a police cruiser and eating was a chore, nothing felt awkward. Reid felt the way he had before Valor had used Reid's personal tragedy as a way to settle a score. It felt like they had been friends for twenty years rather than only months. When he had met Valor last night, he had wanted this back. Still, Reid didn't know if he could or would ever fully trust Valor again, and that was the real problem. Plus, Valor knew all his secrets. That was much harder to swallow than Reid liked. Valor knew he was damaged. There would never be a slow reveal between them—like a period where Valor thought Reid hung the moon and could do no wrong, before being slapped by an ugly past. Valor had been bludgeoned by Reid's past right away. Reid felt like he was likely ugly and broken in Valor's eyes. He didn't know how to stop feeling this way.

"I've missed spending time with you." The confession unexpectedly burst from Reid. He had to start somewhere if he didn't want to feel this way anymore. Reid knew he could go home, never think of Valor again, and that would be the end of this sick feeling in his gut. But Reid would always feel like he failed, if he didn't try to regain the life he had before the media had taken control.

Valor kept his gaze locked on the road while each word he spoke came out haltingly—like he picked through his thoughts. "I've missed you too. While I was really excited to see your show last night, I was also worried that maybe I should stay away. I don't want to be an ugly memory for you, but I also don't want to be an equally ugly constant reminder of things you'd rather forget." Valor blew out a breath— like he thought he was explaining himself badly. "I like you," he said finally, sounding strong as if he found what he meant. "A lot."

Reid stared at the mess in his lap. A smile tugged at his lips as a slow realization grew. "I spent two hours this morning trying to find these croissants because it was important to me that you try them. Obviously, I like you too."

The car came to a stop and Reid realized they were back at Valor's place. Valor put the car in park and sipped his coffee. Reid held his breath while waiting for Valor's dark brown gaze to slide his way. When Valor finally looked at him, Reid thought he would melt to the floor from the hunger in Valor's stare. "Thank you for breakfast. You should let me take you to dinner tonight, so we're even."

"I don't consider us uneven, but I'd still like that."

The happiness in Valor's eyes made Reid's acceptance worthwhile. Reid still didn't know if he made the right decision by allowing Valor back into his life. There was only one way to find out. All Reid knew for sure was something kept drawing him back and making him want more. He had to find out why he couldn't stay away. Reid had a terrible feeling he would regret it if he didn't see Valor again.

SINCE VALOR HADN'T EXPECTED TO SEE REID again, he was more than a little nervous about a dinner date. He wanted to impress Reid, but he also wanted to keep things simple so he wouldn't scare him away. That was why he still stood inside his closet at five minutes until Reid was set to arrive, shirtless while trying to decide which shirt to wear.

The doorbell rang. Valor's gaze moved between a t-shirt he held and a button-down shirt that hung nearby. The doorbell rang again. "Fuck." Valor raced for the door. The last thing he wanted was to ruin his shot because indecisiveness had frozen his feet to the floor. Valor threw open the door.

Reid's gaze dropped to Valor's bare chest before snapping back to his face. "Hi. I'm early. Obviously."

"Sorry. My brain stopped working for a moment when I realized we hadn't talked about where we're going. I didn't know what to wear." Valor's gaze moved down Reid's body, taking in his black pants and soft-looking white sweater. "Damn. You look sexy."

Reid's tempting full lips turned up in the corners into a mouthwatering smile. Valor recognized he needed more clothes right that second before he made an idiot of himself.

He took a step back. "Come in. I'll find a shirt." Valor tried to look everywhere but directly at Reid. Between the blue eyes and his sleek body, Reid was too much of a temptation.

"Take your time. Unless you'd like to wear the shirt you're holding, that is."

Valor barely stopped himself from smacking his own forehead. Jesus. Reid made him into an idiot.

His only excuse was that he had never liked anyone as much as he did Reid. Usually, Valor slept with people and that was the end of things. They had met eight months ago and only shared a few kisses. Reid fucked with his head.

With a blush, Valor pulled the t-shirt on. "Oh, yeah. I forgot."

Reid didn't laugh. In fact, his loving expression sucker-punched Valor. Reid's soft gaze made Valor feel warm all over. "I spend so much brain power trying to remember my lines, I can't remember anything else. You'd be surprised how often I get lost driving to places I've been a hundred times. I walk into rooms and can't recall why. Truly, I'm a mess."

Valor shook his head. He had tried to forget how amazing Reid could be. "Are you in the mood for anything in particular?"

A hint of humor touched Reid's features. He stepped closer. Valor held his breath, waiting to see what Reid would do. His muscles tensed as Reid's palm slid up his chest. As he invaded Valor's space, Valor refused to back down. Whatever Reid wanted, it was his.

Reid fingered the collar of Valor's shirt. "First things first." Reid's voice sounded sexy and breathless. Valor was hooked. Reid shuffled closer. "Your shirt is on inside out and backward."

Heat exploded through Valor's face. He took a step back. "Damn. I—"

Reid overcame him, cutting off his explanation before he could think of one. He nibbled Valor's bottom lip and teased him into a heated kiss. Valor's cock throbbed. Still, he didn't touch Reid. He forced his hands to stay at his sides while Reid held his face and kissed him deeply. Their tongues stroked. Valor's heart raced. He just wanted to be with Reid. Protect him from the world. Valor didn't know how else to explain the emotions that had been growing in his chest from the first moment they met. He felt like he had never known genuine happiness before they met.

Reid pulled away but held on to Valor's face. He swiped the moisture from Valor's lips with his thumbs as his gaze followed the motion. "I'd forgotten how much I love the way you kiss." His gaze lifted, meeting Valor's. The vulnerability in Reid's blue eyes knocked the air from Valor's lungs. "How do you feel about that hibachi place on Lotus Street?"

With a nod, Valor took a step back and quickly

fixed his shirt. "Sounds great." In truth, Valor didn't care where they went as long as Reid kept giving him time. Valor had never met anyone else as amazing. He needed more. Reid had to keep seeing him. Whatever it took.

DINNER PASSED IN A BLINK OF AN EYE. REID HAD forgotten how they talked over each other all the time—like they couldn't get enough of telling each other everything. While there had been a bit of a tussle over the check, Reid had been forced to admit he had said Valor could take him to dinner. By the time they made it back to Valor's, disappointment settled into Reid's chest. He didn't want the night to end, but all things must.

"Would you like to come in for a drink?" When Reid didn't respond right away, Valor held up his hands. "Just a drink. I swear. I'm just not ready for the night to end."

With a laugh, Reid grabbed one of Valor's hands and headed for the door. "Don't swear just yet. I fully expect a goodnight kiss at some point. However, I will accept a drink, as long as it's nonalcoholic. I'm driving, after all."

"Just because I'm a cop doesn't mean I intend to put you in cuffs over one beer."

Reid chuckled at the thought. "Don't threaten me with a good time." As they reached the door, Reid found himself overcome. Like their kiss earlier, Valor didn't touch Reid with anything other than his mouth. Still, Reid felt overwhelmed. With his back against the door and Valor's hands braced on either side of Reid, heat swept over Reid. The first time Reid had kissed Valor several months ago, Valor's hands had been everywhere. It was funny how Reid recognized he wasn't being touched, yet he was still every bit as turned on.

Valor's kiss softened until their lips barely brushed. "There," Valor whispered. "Now you don't have to worry I don't plan to kiss you." Valor let them inside before Reid could think of a response.

With his body still humming with desire, Reid followed Valor through the darkened house to the kitchen. The place smelled like it had been recently cleaned. Valor flipped on the lights in the kitchen and Reid glanced around. The dark gray and white combination of colors were all spotless. The place looked like no one lived there, even though Reid knew Valor spent most of his downtime there.

"You put me to shame. My place is a mess."

Valor flashed him a smile over his shoulder. "I knew you were coming."

And he had cleaned. That was adorable. The kitchen was one long room with a dining area on one end. Reid sat at the oak kitchen table while Valor rummaged around in the fridge.

"I have beer, wine, water, orange juice, and Gatorade. Which will it be?"

"Water is fine." Reid couldn't stop watching Valor's every move. He was a big guy. Normally, Reid steered clear of men with huge muscles. He found those men usually used their size to intimidate. Valor made Reid feel safe—like no one would dare harm him with Valor around.

"Do you go to a gym?" Reid knew it was likely a dumb question, but he wanted to know every detail of Valor's life.

Valor carried their drinks to the table. "No. I used to go to this place across town where police get a discount. But over the years, I've been slowly buying all the equipment I use so I don't have to make the trip. I converted one of my bedrooms into a gym. A lot of people need the motivation of a club setting, but not me. I'm a lot less likely to work out if I have to make a special trip." Valor sat and took a drink. He nodded Reid's way. "You probably get a lot of exercise just from the dance routines in your shows."

Reid nodded. "I do, but I also go to the yoga studio down the street from my house twice a day. They have a short flexibility morning and evening class that keeps me from seizing up after dancing all day. Before starting that, I used to wake up shuffling like an eighty-year-old man."

Valor's eyes flashed with humor. "You're definitely too young for that, but it doesn't wait until you're eighty. The locked muscle shuffle starts closer to forty."

Reid felt like he never stopped smiling when he was with Valor. "Are you saying you're a bit stiff in the mornings?"

With a shake of his head, Valor snorted. His smile never lost a hint of brightness. "I'd like to say I definitely miss the days when I leapt from the bed unhindered, but I don't remember a time like that."

It occurred to Reid that as much as they talked about everything, Valor never talked about his younger days. All his stories were recent. "I know you were born in Hawaii, but I don't think I ever asked how you ended up in L.A."

Valor's smile dimmed. "Baseball. I had a full ride at Fullerton. So I got my degree in criminal justice and stayed."

Even though Reid wanted Valor's smile back, he couldn't stop digging. "Hawaii is an amazing place. Have you ever thought about moving back?"

Valor flashed a pinched smile. "Nope. Not once."

Reid's forehead furrowed at Valor's tone. "Do you not have family there still?"

"Yep. My parents are still there. I usually fly them in around the holidays."

Reid racked his brain, trying to think of any reason Valor wouldn't want to go home. "Do they know you're gay?"

Valor flashed Reid a smile that looked like he tried not to laugh. "I've never said the words to them if that's what you're asking. Not that I think they would care. It's just that I've never had anyone to introduce to them, but I won't hide when that time comes. My parents love me. I'm sure they know, but we don't talk about it. You don't have to worry that I won't tell them about you."

"I'm not worried about that," Reid said with an aggravated huff, even though Reid was flattered that

Valor thought he might need to tell his parents about them. "I'm just trying to get to know you and figure out what drives you. You obviously don't want to go home again and I'm... prying."

A sexy-sounding chuckle rumbled from Valor. He set his beer aside and leaned forward, holding Reid's stare. "Everyone has a past. I also think everyone has this box inside them where they keep the ugly stuff." Reid found himself leaning closer too. He felt less alone in that moment than he had in a long time. Valor kept talking, wrapping him in the warmth of shared experience. "Most of the time, we function normally with that box sealed away deep in the recesses of our minds. But certain places and people, they just peel back the flaps of that box and let all the darkness out. Being back home, and around my parents, it's like that for me." Valor sat back, stealing away Reid's glimpse inside Valor's soul. He kept talking and saved Reid from feeling too bereft. "I minored in theater in college and fell in love with this town. That's another thing that kept me here. L.A. has an artistic culture I didn't have growing up."

Reid was thoroughly distracted. "Did you ever audition for any roles?"

Valor shook his head. "I'm not very good, and I also don't have what it takes to not get a steady paycheck each week. That takes a certain level of faith in your acting abilities that I don't possess. Being here, though." Valor gestured at nothing in particular. "I still get to be immersed in a secondary passion. I can go to the arts center and dream. That's why I can't look away from you." Valor's sudden intensity had Reid drawing a steadying breath. Valor didn't try reining it in. "You have so much talent and drive. Looking at you is like... witnessing history." Valor shook his head. His intensity fell away, and a shy-looking smile touched his lips. "Sorry. I guess that doesn't make sense and probably sounds crazy."

Reid blinked back tears. He had to clear his throat to speak. "No. That's probably the nicest thing anyone has ever said to me. I swing pretty wildly between feeling like I'm a fraud who'll be exposed any moment and thinking I could take over the world. Most of the time, I just accept that I got really, really lucky. Right place. Right time." Reid's words died away as he recalled that Valor knew all his secrets. "Or the wrong one, depending on how you look at things."

Valor made a dismissive gesture and sat forward again. "You shouldn't let anything or anyone invalidate you or your accomplishments. I know you work hard, and I can see you earning your place every time you step out onto that stage. There will always be people who will want you to feel like less so they can feel like more. You're not responsible for how they think and feel. You just have to know the truth in your heart."

With his elbow on the table, Reid leaned his chin on his palm, propping up his head. He was completely immersed in every one of Valor's opinions. "What is the truth?"

Heat poured from Valor's expression, warming Reid's skin. "That you're a star."

Reid rarely felt special anymore. He did in that moment. Valor moved him with his ardor. Reid missed feeling that zeal for his career. Without thought, Reid heard himself confessing as much. "I used to think that was true. There was a time when I really thought I had made it. Now I just feel like I'm an outsider clinging to every role with the tips of my fingers and watching it all slip away."

Pain slashed through Valor's features. "That's my fault."

A sad smile tugged at Reid's lips. He shook his head. "It's not. There's a lot of ugliness behind the curtain of showbusiness that no one ever sees. I used to tell myself that my talent overshadowed what I did to get here. But I'm not so sure anymore."

"I am." Valor truly sounded like he knew. "As long as you keep taking the stage, I'll keep showing up to watch. It's okay for you to doubt yourself, as long as you let me be your confidence. I know you deserve every wonderful thing that's come your way, and I don't doubt there's a lot more to come."

A clock chimed somewhere in the house. Reid checked his watch. "Damn. Where did the night go? You probably have to work tomorrow."

"Yeah. I'd say that's no reason for you to rush off, but I'm sure you have to work tomorrow too with a show going on."

"I do." Reid bit his bottom lip. He really didn't want to leave, but he needed to go. An idea struck. "How do you feel about coming to my house tomorrow night for dinner?"

Valor's eyebrows rose. "You cook too?"

A laugh burst from Reid. "No. Absolutely not. I know how to order takeout."

"Sounds amazing." Damned if Valor didn't sound like he meant it. "I'll walk you to the door."

With his heartbeat pounding in his ears, Reid stood and headed for the door. He could feel Valor following him. His skin tingled with anticipation.

Reid expected Valor to pounce at any second. He wasn't sure how he would react when it happened. Reid turned as they reached the door, bracing himself for Valor's invasion. Instead, he found Valor standing more than a foot away with his hands shoved in his pockets.

"I had an amazing time."

Reid nearly shook his head to clear away the confusion crowding his brain. "Me too," he said instead, hoping to hide his sudden disappointment over Valor's distance.

Valor's gaze shifted away, seeming suddenly nervous. "I know I already claimed my goodnight kiss, but would it be okay if—"

Reid snagged Valor's t-shirt and towed him forward. He claimed Valor's mouth, cutting off the question. Valor didn't exactly stay stiff beneath Reid's kiss. His mouth chased Reid like a man starved for attention, but he never removed his hands from his pockets. Reid tried not to let that bother him. After all, Valor was a gentleman. Reid just kind of wished Valor wasn't quite so much the respectful date. It had been a long time since anyone held him. Reid missed the warmth. Still, Reid bowed out without complaint. He understood he wasn't the catch he had been before his past had come to light.

Reid could hardly expect Valor to find him sexually attractive now. Valor was a cop. Reid would always be the victim to him. It was disheartening, but Reid had to let that go. This undesired state was his new reality. Reid was pretty good at feeling empty.

THREE

THERE WAS a genuine possibility that Valor might explode from unquenched desire or rub his dick completely off. Either one was only a date or two more away from happening. Every single night for over a month, Valor had been meeting Reid for dinner, taking turns between their houses. Each night ended with a heated kiss where Valor kept his hands to himself, and he was slowly dying. He didn't know what sign he expected to see, but he knew Reid would let him know when the time had come to make a move. For now, Reid was killing him.

Tonight was his night to handle dinner. Since he was a little late getting off, he had already decided they would go out. Valor didn't have time to shower and cook before Reid got there. As Valor pulled into his driveway and parked next to a black Porsche Panamera, he knew immediately he wouldn't get that shower. A bright smile pulled at his lips as he leapt from his patrol car. Sergio Costa sat on Valor's front porch, looking like a superstar. The young Hispanic that Valor had met as a homeless teen had enormous diamonds in each ear and a thick gold watch. His white pants and muscle shirt made his skin look darker than usual. His black hair was styled to perfection. Even his smile looked like a million dollars.

Sergio stood as Valor jogged up the front steps. "There he is," Sergio said, grabbing Valor's hand and pulling him in for a one-armed hug.

Valor couldn't be happier to see Sergio. "It's been too long. What brings you by?"

Sergio shrugged and reclaimed his seat on the park bench sitting on Valor's porch. His dark green eyes flashed Valor's way. "I saw on the TV that you're dating celebrities now. I had to stop by and talk about that."

Valor tried biting back a smile as he moved to sit next to Sergio on the bench. "We should talk about you instead. You're all famous now. I actually caught one of your soccer matches live a few months back.

And what about that shy little redhead I saw you with not too long ago? Where are you hiding him?"

Sergio's smile fell. "Nah, I didn't come here to talk about me. It's not right to turn things around on me like that. I'm not the kid anymore. I get to pry in your business now."

"Were you ever a kid?"

Sergio looked away and shrugged. "Sure. Play that game. His name was Lee and we've been done for a couple of months now."

Valor was always here to talk when it came to one of the kids he had mentored in a community project that was close to his heart. They were his kids. He never lost touch. "I'm sorry to hear that. What happened?"

A bitter-looking smile touched Sergio's lips. "Oh, you know. The usual. It started with this one guy on the team asking me to tell him hi. I thought it was a dig at my sexuality, especially when it kept happening. It seemed like everyone pretended they knew Lee after one meeting and liked him a little too much for strangers. Lee always acted so shy that people like to take care of him. Some of the guys were really nice about it, so I kind of thought maybe they just thought he was as awesome as I did."

Valor groaned. "How many of the other guys was he fucking?"

Sergio made a wild gesture, as if really getting into the story. "All of them, man. Like everyone I introduced him to. Turns out, after meeting them, he would slide up into their DMs and get all sexy. It was a big joke to all the guys."

Valor winced. "Damn. Now you're stuck playing with them."

With a shrug, Sergio visibly tried to go back to looking carefree. "It's okay. Like, I make a lot of money now and I'm not a dumbass the way they are. The streets raised me. I know how to be safe. I never touch anyone without protection, and he gave like five of them the herp dog."

A laugh burst from Valor. "Poetic justice, I suppose." Valor shook his head. A snort escaped him. He gave Sergio's shoulder a pat. Valor couldn't avoid talking about his life after Sergio poured out his heart like that. "I like him."

Sergio looked over and held Valor's stare at the confession. In that moment, he looked more like the too quiet boy Valor had met a decade ago and less like the famous soccer player he had become. "Is he worth liking?"

Valor nodded. He knew all his boys trusted him

and his sixth sense about people. "He's a good person who's been handed a lot of terrible things to handle. I like talking to him."

A loud snort escaped Sergio. "Don't play. I've seen him in movies. You like to talk," Sergio mocked and snorted again.

Before Valor could reaffirm his claim, Reid's car turned into the driveway. He parked behind Valor's patrol car and stepped out. The passenger side opened as well.

While Valor strained to see who Reid had brought along for the ride, Sergio started playfully hitting Valor's arm. "Look at you. It's really him. You're really dating a famous dude. Player."

Reid's gaze moved between them, but his smile was every bit as genuine as ever. "Hey. Sorry I'm late."

Valor was sufficiently distracted from the tiny blond guy following on Reid's heels. "Hi. It's fine. As you can see, I haven't even had time to change out of my uniform."

"That's my fault," Sergio said, jumping to his feet and holding his hand out for Reid to shake. "I'm Sergio. Your man helped raise me. He's a real hero."

Valor couldn't look away from the sweet smile Reid wore. He barely stopped himself from sighing.

Reid was just so damn beautiful. "I know. He saves everyone he meets. I'm Reid."

Sergio nodded. He leaned to the side, trying to see the tiny guy hiding behind Reid. "I know. I've seen you in movies. Who's your friend?"

Reid stepped aside, exposing an adorable guy who looked like he wished the ground would open and swallow him whole. "This is Tobin. He's a pastry chef. I'm hoping Valor will take us to The Back Porch tonight and make an introduction to the owner."

Tobin gave a slight wave. He couldn't have looked more uncomfortable if he tried. "Hi. Sorry to ruin date night. Reid kind of shoved me in the car. Some might even say he kidnapped me."

"Damn. That's gangster," Sergio said, smiling brightly. "My car is right there if you need saving."

Tobin dropped his gaze to the ground, but he wasn't quick enough to hide his blush. "I'm good. Reid drags me around a lot."

Reid rolled his eyes. "Somebody has to, or you'd stay locked up in your apartment every day. You'll never get new clients by staying home."

Valor's cheeks ached, making him realize how bright his smile had become. "We definitely have to head to The Back Porch tonight. Even if Wrecker isn't there, he lives nearby. We'll get this new partnership going. What do you say, Sergio? Would you like to go too? You're young and single," Valor tacked on since Sergio kept eyeing Tobin like his next meal.

Sergio stepped off the front porch. "I wish I could, man. Work stuff calls, but..." He turned and eyed Tobin a little too close to be misunderstood. "... it was really nice meeting you. I don't spend a lot of time at The Back Porch, but if you got some partnership going on there, I might have to start making the trip."

Tobin lifted his chin for a half a second to meet Sergio's stare before his gaze went back to the ground. "It was nice meeting you too."

Sergio bit his plump bottom lip and shook his head as he stared a hole in the top of Tobin's head. "Maybe I'll run into you again sometime."

Tobin sneaked a peek at Sergio again. "Keep hanging around these guys and I'm sure you'll see me kidnapped again."

With a smirk, Sergio walked backward toward his car for a second while still checking out Tobin.

Valor shook his head at the guy's confidence. Sergio had always bordered on cocky when he felt comfortable around people or when he was on the field. It was a trait that had served him well. Tobin didn't seem to be immune. Reid and Valor exchanged a knowing look. They would have to make sure the pair crossed paths again. That was the thing about being in love. It made people want everyone else to feel the same way.

———

VALOR HAD BEEN ADORABLY PATIENT THROUGH introducing Tobin to Wrecker. Tobin didn't have many friends because he was so quiet, introverted, and shy. He was the kind of person who needed extroverts to adopt him or no one noticed him. Reid knew Valor would be immediately protective of him —the way he was with everyone the least bit in need. Tobin needed friends more than most for reasons Reid couldn't share. It wasn't his place, but he was ridiculously happy to see Valor working so hard on Tobin's behalf.

By the time they dropped Tobin off at his apartment and were alone at Valor's house, Reid was more than ready to climb him like a tree. Still, he also felt like he owed Valor an apology for hijacking their date night. "Sorry I sprang the whole Tobin thing on you without warning. We were talking and I saw my chance to kidnap him."

Valor tucked Reid's hair behind his ear. His gaze followed the motion. "Never apologize to me for helping someone. I'm here for that."

Reid flattened his palms against Valor's chest and walked him backward toward the couch. "Speaking of helping people, would you like to tell me how you know Sergio Costa and why he's calling you a hero?" Reid pushed, forcing Valor to sit before crawling into his lap.

Valor wrapped his arms around Reid's waist and shifted his weight to one leg, settling in. "I wasn't aware you knew who Sergio is."

Valor rolled his eyes. "I'm not completely sports ignorant."

With a shrug, Valor still tried to blow off Reid's question. "Sergio was just trying to make me look good by calling me a hero."

"I seriously doubt that. You don't need help to impress me, so what's the story?"

"I didn't really do anything," Valor said, sounding like he truly believed that. "There's a community outreach project where police can volunteer. We just play sports with the kids and kind of mentor them while trying to foster trust. Sergio was a homeless teen with a ton of talent. I just helped him get in front of the right eyes. He got a scholarship that got him off the streets before getting picked up by a pro team. Like I said, I didn't really do anything. He already had all the talent and put in the hard work. I was just lucky enough to have met him."

Reid shook his head. "So humble while always saving everyone."

Valor leaned his head back against the couch and eyed Reid. "Caring about other people is nothing to brag about, especially when it comes to kids. It's the adults of the world's job to keep kids safe. If I can help, I will. You're bragging about me while you're doing the same thing for Tobin."

If Valor wanted to talk about Reid, Reid would give him more than he could handle. "I'm just helping out a friend. But if you're determined to talk about me, then I'll bite. Are you refusing to touch me because of my past?"

Valor blinked hard, as if Reid broke his brain. He didn't respond right away, telling Reid everything he needed to know. He started to climb from Valor's lap, but Valor held tight. "In an oversimplified way, yes." Reid held still, but Valor's honesty hurt. Luckily, Valor didn't let his disappointment grow. Valor held his stare like he would talk about anything Reid wanted to discuss. "You're wanted, so please don't get that in your head. But I don't want to do anything you're not ready to do. I've just been waiting for you to let me know."

It was odd. Reid's life had been such a mess for so long now that he had forgotten he could make the first move too. He was slightly scared of his decision-making ability. Reid didn't know if he trusted himself anymore. Coming to terms with his molestation had undermined everything beautiful about sex for him. He didn't want to be like this.

"Stop."

Reid blinked. "Stop what?"

A sad-looking smile touched Valor's lips. "Stop trying to force yourself to be ready for something when you're not. I'm happy. No rush."

Frustration nearly choked Reid. "But that's not true. This isn't about not being ready." His shoulders fell. "I don't know how to explain it. You're very much wanted." A growl rose in Reid's throat. "Goddamn it. I want you to stop thinking I'm fucked up and you need to be the hero." Reid pushed from Valor's lap and headed for the door. He was pretty damn positive he was in love with Valor, but Valor would never see him as an equal. Reid didn't want to be Valor's fucking project. He wanted to be in a real, adult, and equal relationship. Reid didn't feel like they matched.

As Reid grabbed the doorknob, Valor overcame him. With his hand flattened against the door, Valor held it closed, stopping Reid from getting away. Before Reid could snap, Valor's lips brushed Reid's nape. His hard body molded against Reid's back. Reid's forehead hit the door. His breath left him in a heavy pant as Valor's mouth moved to where Reid's shoulder met his neck. Valor's hands moved from the door to gently cupping Reid's throat and urging him back while his teeth and tongue played with Reid's ear. Goosebumps skated across Reid's skin. His entire body went on alert.

"Holy shit." The breathless curse slipped from Reid as his cock stirred.

Valor's hand slid down the front of Reid's body and cupped Reid's erection through his jeans. Since they had started dating in earnest, Valor hadn't really touched Reid. He was now. Reid thought his body would go up in flames. A whimper escaped Reid as he moved against Valor's hand.

"I don't think you're fucked up," Valor said against Reid's ear. "I think you're too much of a temptation and I need to take things slow." He popped the button loose on Reid's jeans and slowly, tooth by tooth, slid Reid's zipper down. "Once I have you, I know it's all I'll ever think about anymore. I'm already half insane from craving you all the time and I haven't touched you yet." Valor's hand slipped inside Reid's underwear. His fingers encircled Reid's cock. A ragged-sounding breath caressed Reid's ear as Valor stroked and weakened Reid's knees. "Goddamn. I have never wanted anything or anyone as much as I do you."

"Then do it," Reid taunted. The words sounded wicked—like they came from someone else. Wanting Valor had stripped away all sense of self-preservation. The room spun as Valor turned Reid in his arms and went on the attack. He tugged and pulled at Reid's clothes, stripping him bare while Reid could only pant for air.

"Goddamn, you're beautiful." The harsh whisper barely penetrated the sound of Reid's heartbeat thumping in his ears. Valor's mouth crashed down onto Reid's. As their tongues fought, Reid climbed Valor until his legs were wrapped around Valor's waist. Valor squeezed his ass, kneading as he walked down the hall with Reid wrapped around him like a monkey. Reid didn't pay attention to anything they passed. His focus couldn't be budged from the body against him.

A cool mattress touched Reid's back. A gasp escaped Reid at the contrast against his heated skin. He felt like he was on fire with Valor's lips, teeth, and tongue finding every place he could reach on Reid's body. Valor went up onto his knees long enough to peel off his shirt and toss it away. Reid caught a glimpse of Valor's hard chest before Valor was back on the attack. He kissed a path down Reid's body. All Reid could do was squirm beneath him, seeking relief from the all-consuming lust. Then his dick was in Valor's mouth. A loud whimper escaped Reid. He dug his heels into the mattress as he pushed his hips upward, seeking more. Reid needed release from the madness. Valor's tongue slid along Reid's length, driving him crazy. Reid clawed at Valor's shoulders as he fucked Valor's mouth. He moved faster. Orgasm was a breath away. Valor moved away, dragging a cry of denial from Reid. He was so close. Reid almost grabbed his cock and finished himself off, but cool, wet fingers stretched his asshole and distracted him. There was a slight crinkle of plastic ripping. That was all the warning Reid got before a much larger part of Valor pushed its way inside. Valor shoved. Reid saw stars. His entire body convulsed as Valor hit the right spot and sent him flying. Cries tore from Reid's throat. He could hear Valor speaking, but he couldn't make out the words. The ecstasy stole his ability to decipher any human language.

Valor cried out against his ear, bringing Reid back down to reality and making him wonder how long Valor had broken his mind. He didn't know how Valor could have come because Reid had been a useless blob of jelly after his powerful orgasm. There was no way Valor had enjoyed that to Reid's mind, but there was no denying the harsh breaths against his ear and the way Valor shook in his arms.

"Fuck." The harsh whisper against his skin had Reid's eyes falling closed. Valor kissed his neck. "You've done it now. You'll never get rid of me."

A chuckle burst from Reid. His arms tightened around Valor. "Thank god." Reid had never meant anything more. Valor made him feel everything: turned on, safe, loved, and ridiculously happy. Reid didn't want to lose him. He wanted this relationship like he hadn't with anyone else before. Reid also knew he wasn't easy to love, but Valor was strong enough for the job. Thank god he wanted it, because Reid would likely test him for the rest of his life. Reid was dumb like that.

VALOR COULDN'T BREATHE. BEING WITH REID was everything he had expected and more. He was so fucking glad that Reid had come quickly because Valor had not lasted long. All the waiting for Reid to be ready had gotten the best of him. Just being inside Reid had been enough to send him over the edge. Now he couldn't move away. He needed the sensation of their racing hearts thumping against each other. Valor swallowed back words that it seemed way too soon to say.

Instead, he kissed the spot beneath Reid's ear, giving his lips something to do. "Mhmm. I love this spot."

A winded chuckle caressed his shoulder as Reid placed a kiss there. "That's a pretty innocuous spot."

"Not to me." Valor kept brushing his lips down Reid's neck until he reached his shoulder. "Will you stay the night and let me make you breakfast?"

"I'm not sure I could move even if I wanted."

Valor rolled to his side but didn't set Reid free. He draped one leg over Reid's body so he couldn't get away. Reid turned his head. They held each other's stare. Valor wondered if he looked as besotted as he felt. He wasn't sure he cared.

"Being with you makes me feel like I must've gone right in a past life."

Valor sucked in a deep breath at Reid's words. He should have been the one to say that. "You're incredibly out of my league."

Reid shook his head. His throat moved, as if he swallowed hard. "I'm not. I'm just some guy."

"Not to me." Even to Valor's ears, he sounded like the claim came from his soul.

For what felt like forever, Reid stared at him in silence. When he finally spoke, his voice came out low, as if confessing a secret. "I love spending time with you. I've never been this happy."

Valor kissed Reid because he had to taste those words. While they weren't the ones he really wanted to hear, Reid's words had been damn close. Reid's confession made Valor feel like they were headed toward forever. Valor had never wanted that before Reid. Now he couldn't stop thinking about settling down permanently. This was where he wanted to spend the rest of his life, holding Reid.

Valor pulled away and brushed noses with Reid. "Let me throw this condom away, and then we can take a long, hot shower together before I carry you back to bed. Sound good?"

As Reid nodded, looking so young and trusting,

Valor experienced a moment of complete terror from nowhere. He had to keep Reid safe. Not physically, even though he fully intended to do that too, but mentally. Valor understood the doubt and silent suffering Reid went through alone. He couldn't let the love of his life hurt anymore. Valor needed to ensure the rest of Reid's life was nothing but laughter and joy. That was Valor's job now. He couldn't fail. At Reid's age, Valor had been scarred too badly to give his heart to anyone. If Reid was the same, then there was no hope for a future between them. Valor couldn't have that. He had finally healed and found love. Valor would do the same for Reid. He had to, because losing Reid wasn't an option. Valor's sanity couldn't handle it. They had to make it. Valor couldn't live with any other outcome.

FOUR

VALOR: *Someone called out sick. I have to cover their shift.*

Reid: *Disappointed, but I'll live... maybe.*

Valor: *The guilt. I can't take it.*

Reid: *I'm joking. It's fine. Maybe I'll practice my breaking and entering while you're working and fall asleep in your bed.*

Valor: ***mock gasp** But I thought you were so innocent.*

Reid: *Seriously, though. I miss you already.*

Valor: *I miss you too. There's a spare key out back. It's beneath the wheel of my BBQ grill. Please use it any time you'd like. I'd love to come home to you.*

Reid: *I might take you up on that.*

REID: *I STILL CAN'T BELIEVE IT'S BEEN THREE weeks since I've seen you. Have you met someone else while I've been working? Am I forgotten yet?*

Valor: *I know you're joking. You're irreplaceable. I knew when we started dating there would be times when you would be gone. You have nothing to fear. I'm like an old faithful dog. I'll be sitting on the front porch, waiting for you to get home. Just don't find someone younger and forget me.*

Reid: ***snort** I'd rather have an old faithful dog than an untrained pup any day.*

Valor: *Are you saying you have me trained?*

Reid: *That's not what I meant.*

Valor: *I know. I'm just giving you a hard time, but you're right. You do have me trained. I'm up and ready to beg at just the thought of you.*

Reid: *You're ridiculous.*

Valor: *I know, but you wouldn't have me any other way.*

Reid: *I'd have you absolutely any way I could get you.*

Valor: *I'm so ready for you to be home.*

VALOR: MOM'S FLIGHT IS COMING IN AT SIX. SHE won't let me pick her up, because she's always been stubborn like that. So, since she's coming in so late, I gave her your address. That way, she can come straight to your place and we can eat dinner at a decent time. Is that okay?

Reid: That works for me. It'll probably take a good hour or more for her to get out of the airport and get to my place through rush hour traffic. That's if she lands on time. No one wants to wait until ten to eat. You two could stay with me, if you want.

Valor: You're amazing, but no. Trust me. You really don't want that. Mom likes to take over people's houses. You wouldn't get any peace.

Reid: I don't mind. I want her to like me.

Valor: You have nothing to worry about. She was a bit surprised to learn I'm dating a man, but I've never introduced her to anyone. So she already thinks you're perfect and is already planning to talk to you about adopting her some grandbabies.

Reid: Yikes.

Valor: Exactly. Stop worrying about the wrong things. LOL!

REID'S HOUSE WAS SURROUNDED BY A HUGE brick and wrought-iron fence. It looked imposing and hid the gorgeous house from view. Like all celebrities, there was no mailbox or numbers marking the property, giving clues to who lived there. It was just a gate with a code. If a person didn't already know who lived there and the numbers to pass through, then no one saw beyond that point. Each time Valor punched the correct buttons for the gate to swing wide, he felt special—like he had passed a test. He saw behind a curtain that normal people didn't get to view. Being with Reid was the most amazing thing that had ever happened to him. Valor never stopped feeling blessed.

As Valor circled the pebbled concrete driveway to park at Reid's front door, he marveled anew at the beauty of the place. The driveway had been sealed with glowing pebbles that lit up like twinkling stars, guiding the way to a white stone house that stood bright even in the dark. Valor loved the place. Not because it was gorgeous and probably cost several million dollars, but because Reid was inside. After five months of dating steadily on top of eight months of pining, Valor was more than in love. He was certain Reid was the one. Christmas was only a couple of weeks away and Valor had already bought a ring. He recognized he would likely get shot down. If so, he would still keep loving Reid, but the answer would always be no if he didn't ask.

In a way, it felt weird being poised to propose when they hadn't exchanged I love yous yet. Valor knew the truth, though. He could see and feel Reid's love every minute of the day. No one else had gotten an introduction to his mom. Valor was more than a little nervous about that. In fact, he was more worried about Reid meeting his mom than he was about popping the question. He had more to lose from one than the other.

The front door opened before Valor could ring the bell. Reid stood in the open doorway. Light surrounded him like a halo. In an off-white sweater and black jeans, he looked like a dream come true. Valor picked up his pace, needing to touch him. His lips tingled with anticipation of Reid's kiss.

"What time is it?" Even Valor heard the slight growl in his voice.

Reid checked his watch. "It's six thirty."

"Thank god," Valor breathed, closing the distance between them. "We have time." He didn't give Reid a chance to ask any questions. Valor swept Reid from his feet and tossed him over his shoulder while kicking the door closed behind him. Reid's laughter made the move worthwhile. But Valor wasn't joking. He needed to taste Reid's skin. His bad nerves were showing themselves in the only way he could control.

Valor didn't stop moving until he could toss Reid on the couch. While Reid still bounced, looking stunned, Valor pounced. He captured Reid's lips while going to work on Reid's jeans. "I want you in my mouth. Please fuck my face," Valor begged between kisses. It wasn't even about lust. Valor needed the connection. He had to know he brought Reid an ounce of the joy Reid gave him every day. Otherwise, his lungs might collapse. Maybe that didn't make sense to anyone else, but Valor felt it. Valor needed to deserve Reid, because he didn't. He really, really didn't. Reid just didn't realize it yet.

Reid went hard in Valor's hand. Valor sucked in a deep breath at the sensation. He stroked as he swiped his tongue one last time against Reid's before pulling away. Valor didn't play. He went straight for the prize. Without any hesitation, Valor swallowed Reid's cock. Reid's hips left the couch.

"Holy shit. That's good."

Valor knew he had gone completely over the edge. He couldn't stop himself. Not telling Reid every second of the day how much he loved him was making Valor insane. He had to go somewhere with all the pent-up adoration. Valor sucked and tugged, needing cum to fill his mouth. He craved the sound of Reid's cries. Reid scratched at Valor's shoulders. Whimpering filled the air as Reid pumped against Valor's mouth. Valor used every skill he possessed to pleasure Reid. Reid's body stiffened. Valor sucked hard. A cry tore through the room as hot cum hit the back of Valor's throat. He swallowed, going wild on Reid's dick. Valor wanted all of it. He needed Reid to glow all night from this moment.

When the madness ebbed, Valor found himself panting. Moving slower, he made his way back to Reid's mouth. Their kiss was slow and gentle. Reid's fingertips toyed with Valor's nape—like he couldn't stop touching him. The backs of Valor's eyes burned. He had found his home here with Reid. In a few brief moments, his mom would be here to ruin this, and Valor hated that. He despised the way he had been feeling for the past month while planning this visit. While it was true that Valor had never dated anyone long enough to introduce them to his parents, there was a myriad of reasons he stayed away from Hawaii and them. Now Reid had invited all that mess into his home. This night might end up a nightmare. Valor wanted to cling to the love before the ugliness pushed its way in.

A chiming cut through the silence.

Reid pulled away, looking panicked. "That's the front gate. Your mom's car must be here."

Valor brushed his lips across Reid's one last time and helped set his clothes to right. He smiled and reassured Reid a hundred times that he looked fine and everything would go great. The entire time, Valor memorized Reid's face, knowing this might be the last time Reid looked at him with total love and trust. He just had to get through one night. Valor could do it, and then he would make sure Reid didn't set eyes on his mom again this entire trip.

MALIA TURNED OUT TO BE AN AMAZING LADY who talked more than Valor and Reid combined. Reid had been a nervous wreck about meeting Valor's mom, especially when Valor's father had declined to visit. Valor claimed he didn't feel up to traveling, but Reid wasn't dumb. He knew he was bombshell news to Valor's parents no matter how much everyone pretended otherwise. Apparently, Valor dating a famous guy didn't outweigh the fact that Reid was still a man. Reid tried not to let that get to him. After all, his mom had pimped him out as a child to make him famous. Any mom at all was better than his.

"Thank you for dinner, Reid. You are a good boy."

Reid bit the inside of his cheek to keep from laughing. "You're very welcome. I'm just happy to finally meet you." Reid kept washing dishes to hide his nervousness. Even though they had been talking all night, this was the first time Malia had cornered him alone. Valor was busy taking her bags to his truck. They would only be without him for a few minutes, but Valor's absence strained Reid's nerves to the limit. He didn't know how to behave with an actual mom. Hell, he was washing dishes because she expected him to, even though he had a cleaning service.

Malia patted his arm. "I'm so glad you're a part of my Valor's life. You are overcoming so much in the public eye right now." Horror nearly swelled Reid's throat closed. He hadn't known she knew anything about all that, but Malia wasn't finished. "Don't look like that. You're exactly what my angel needs. After his big scandal back home, he never faced down the gossips the way you have. You've shown a lot of grace and I think watching you will help bring Valor home. At least for visits anyhow. We're not getting any younger and the flight is feeling longer all the time, as you can see by Kaeo not making the trip. Plus, it would be nice to see my son more than once a year."

Reid nodded along with no clue what she meant about Valor's scandal. He decided to move past it and pepper Valor later. "Maybe I can convince Valor to make the trip after my latest show ends. If you think Kaeo would be okay with me visiting." Reid bit his bottom lip, hoping he didn't go too far.

Malia threw her arms up. "Are you kidding me? He has watched *Secret of the Mystery Baker* so many times, I am sick. When he learned Valor and you are dating, I had to pry the phone from Kaeo's hand to stop him from nagging Valor with questions. He was sad he couldn't come, but his heart is not so good anymore. The flight is hard on him."

Reid nodded. He would try harder to get Valor to see his family. "I'll drag him home soon for a visit. By summer, at the latest."

"Are you two conspiring against me?" Valor appeared behind Reid and dragged him back against his chest. His lips brushed Reid's nape, making his eyes fall closed.

"Would I do such a thing?"

"You? Probably. But Mom? Definitely."

Malia smacked Valor's arm and headed for the door. "I need to sit down. My old hips are killing me."

The moment they were alone, Reid killed the water, dried his hands, and turned in Valor's arms. Valor's eyes hooded as Reid's hands slid up his chest. Reid's heart skipped a beat. He was ridiculously in love, and he wanted to say it, but sometimes Reid still questioned his judgment. Instead, Reid decided to use the moment alone to pry.

"Your mom says she hopes you watching me handle my scandal will help you deal with yours."

Valor winced and immediately stepped out of Reid's hold. "Sorry about that. She has no filter."

Reid waved off Valor's apology. "Since I wasn't aware you had a scandal, my curiosity is at an all-time high."

With a roll of his eyes, Valor dismissed Reid's attempt to get more information. "She just wants me to move home and you're the first person I've introduced her to. She hopes we'll get married, move in next door, and adopt all those grandbabies I was telling you about. Don't worry about it. She's just being a mom."

There was more to the story, but Reid didn't

know how to get to it without driving a wedge between them. Valor was already pulling away. Reid could feel it happening. "Okay."

Valor rubbed the back of his neck and glanced around. "I hate to run, but I'm really tired and I have the early shift tomorrow. Plus, I need to get Mom settled in."

"Sure." Reid knew when he was getting blown off. No matter what shift Valor worked, he never left this early. "You have to go, get some sleep, and all that. I understand." Actually, he only partially got it. On one hand, Malia probably was jet-lagged and ready to rest. On the other, Reid couldn't understand why he felt Valor closing off—like he didn't intend to come back after Reid's question. Reid tried not to show his disappointment. He had been in a panic, planning this night, since learning Malia would be visiting a month ago. Reid felt like Valor was purposely rushing his mother away—like he didn't want Reid interacting with her too much.

A small smile touched Valor's lips. "Thank you for all this." He motioned toward where Malia had disappeared.

Reid shrugged. "You have no reason to thank me. I enjoyed myself. Hopefully, I'll get to steal your mom for a day of shopping or something while she's here."

Valor's smile turned brittle. "Sure."

Damn. Valor really didn't want Reid alone with his mom for whatever reason. There was no sense in digging now. He invaded Valor's space, teasing him with light kisses before moving back, dragging a playful smile from Valor.

"Tease," Valor whispered, backing him against the counter.

An inner sigh of relief rang through Reid's head. Valor looked fine. It was possible he had overthought things. "Maybe, but I'm not opposed to pleasing if you decide to sneak away and visit me alone."

"Mhmm," Valor hummed. "I just might do that." He kissed the side of Reid's neck and lingered. Reid's eyes fell closed as Valor's arms tightened around him. "You're amazing. I don't tell you that often enough."

Joy filled Reid to overflowing. "Only because I've never been so happy. I want you to be every bit as happy with me."

"I've never been more ecstatic in my life. Every day is another opportunity to be with you."

Jesus. He was so in love, he was bursting with it. As much as he didn't want Valor to go, he knew

Valor would be back the second he could get away. They were headed toward forever. Reid felt that in his bones. Meeting Valor's mom was the confirmation Reid needed. He would ask Valor to marry him at Christmas. They were meant to be.

INSIDE, VALOR WAS IN A FROTHY RAGE. His scandal. He couldn't fucking believe his mom had said that to Reid. For the past month, while they had been planning this visit, that had been one of his biggest fears. Considering damn near everything he had worried about had come true thus far, he should have known this one would too. He should have skipped this yearly visit. His father's reaction to learning about Reid should have been his first clue to cancel. Between his dad saying Valor's scandal and L.A. living had turned him gay, and his mom using those fucking words with Reid, Valor was already done. His mom was always talking about her future grandbabies. Well, she could forget it. If all parents acted like Reid's and his, then fuck that noise. Valor never wanted to join their ranks.

"I really love Reid. He's a delightful boy. You

should get him to come with us tomorrow on our bus tour."

Valor kept his eyes locked on the road. His grip tightened on the steering wheel. "Reid can't go on a bus tour; he would get mobbed. Not that it matters. He's a busy guy. He'll likely be working most of the week."

She would not be seeing Reid again, since she had already proven herself untrustworthy.

"Oh. I didn't think about that. You two probably don't get to go out too many places. Does he get his picture taken by the paparazzi all the time? Does he have a bodyguard? If so, is he single?"

Valor rubbed his forehead. "You're married already... to my dad," he reminded her, trying to cling to a respectful voice. She was still his mom, no matter how angry he was at the moment.

"I know. I was just asking."

She sounded so deflated that a hint of guilt settled into Valor's chest. He tried harder to let the scandal comment go. "No, he doesn't have a bodyguard. This is L.A. and a ton of celebrities live here. Some still do have bodyguards, but Reid doesn't. He has me. Still, going on a bus tour meant for tourists to see celebrity homes is the kind of thing that would be hell for Reid."

She managed to hold her silence long enough for Valor to think he might survive this visit. Then it was over. "Reid says you two will visit in the summer. I'll make sure your father behaves. He is getting better. You gave him a shock, to be sure, but he is coming to terms."

A steady breath filled Valor's lungs as he counted to ten inside his head. He tried to sound calm. "Tell him not to bother tolerating us. We won't be visiting this summer."

"Reid will get you there."

Valor ground his back teeth. He regretted this visit more and more by the second. Loving Reid had gotten to him. He had let himself get carried away with the idea of a normal life. One where he could introduce his boyfriend to his parents and start planning a future. Valor had forgotten this part. The part where his parents were awful. He wouldn't let this happen again. Once this visit came to an end, it would be the last. He would marry Reid and make a new family. It didn't matter that his parents weren't the root cause of why he couldn't return to Hawaii. They hadn't behaved as parents should since the worst moment of his life. He had been failed by them. Over the years, he had tried to forgive and forget. In one night, his mom had reminded him of why he couldn't. Reid was Valor's future. Valor would keep his eyes locked ahead from now on. The rest of his life would be reserved for only Reid. It was for the best. No one here looked at him like the pitiful victim... or worse. It was long past the time he should have cut all ties. Next week, he would do better.

FIVE

REID: *Do you think your mom would like to hang out with me today while you're working? You could come over when you get off and I could take us to dinner.*

Valor: *I'm sure she would love that. Maybe tomorrow. She left for some Hollywood bus tour thing early this morning.*

Reid: *Oh. Okay. That stinks. I could have given her a behind-the-scenes tour.*

REID: *Would your mom and you like to go to lunch? I could pick her up and meet you somewhere on your lunch hour.*

Valor: *I'm sorry. She's doing more touristy crap today and I'm working through lunch.*

Reid: *Okay. Maybe tomorrow.*

REID: *MAY I TAKE YOUR MOM AND YOU TO LUNCH today?*

Valor: *I took an early lunch and Mom is having lunch with Dawson and Milo today.*

Reid: *All right. Understood.*

Valor: *What's understood?*

Reid: *Nothing. Have a good day at work.*

REID WAS BEYOND TIRED OF GETTING BLOWN OFF by Valor. He didn't understand what was happening between them. For months, they had been perfect, spending every free minute together. Reid had thought, all the way up until he asked about Valor's past, that they were golden. Getting introduced to Valor's mom was like passing some sort of initiation, and—apparently—he had failed. Valor was short answering his texts and avoiding him like he had been dumped while he wasn't looking. Reid's mind was a mess. Everything hurt. He had been offered a spot on a Broadway event that he didn't feel like he should pass up, but Reid also didn't feel like he could leave while their relationship seemed so up in the air. The show's producer had given Reid twenty-four hours to think it over before he planned to move on to the next name on his list. Reid wanted the part, but he loved Valor. He didn't know how to leave while they were having problems he didn't understand. He had to know what was going on.

Without any hope of dragging answers from Valor, Reid went to the next best source. He felt sick as he rang the doorbell on the gray stone building. Even though the place was a gallery, it wasn't open to the public most days and he hadn't called ahead. He shouldn't be here. Nothing good could come of this. Milo opened the door, looking closed off to anything Reid had to say. Reid couldn't blame him. "Hi." Even Reid heard the awkwardness in his voice. Reid held out the bottle of wine he had brought. "My mom used to say I should never drop by without a gift. I guess, in this case, it's a peace offering."

Milo accepted the bottle, but he didn't speak.

The discomfort grew. Reid shifted from foot to foot. Milo's silver eyes were very disconcerting. Reid found himself rambling. "I know that you're barely stopping yourself from slamming the door in my face. You have every right to do so, but—with your permission—I'd really like to talk to Dawson. It's about Valor," Reid rushed to add so Milo wouldn't get the wrong idea. "If you say no, I will honor that, but this is really important." Reid blew out a sigh, feeling like an idiot. "It would have to be, wouldn't it?" Reid's muttered question was more for himself.

"If you had told me what my mom had done the first time we met, instead of trying to hurt us, I would've helped you."

Reid's throat immediately swelled. His eyes burned, forcing him to drop his gaze to his feet. He never expected words to hurt as badly as Milo's did. Milo had such a soulful voice mixed with a hint of innocence. He made Reid want to protect him from the ugliness of reality. But now, he had to be one hundred percent genuine if he hoped to move past this.

Reid took a steadying breath and met Milo's stare. He tried not to let his voice crack, but it was impossible. "I don't know how to trust people. Your mom, and mine, taught me a lot of hard life lessons, but I'm trying."

Milo dropped his gaze and eyed the bottle Reid

had given him. "Dawson is putting together a giant-sized canvas for me in the studio. I'm sure he would love a distraction from cursing my name." Milo took a step back and let Reid pass.

Reid swiped his palms on his jeans. "Thank you. Maybe I can help."

With a wave, Milo directed him toward an open doorway on their right. Definite cursing and banging floated from the room. "Just follow the rage. I'll bring you both something to drink."

As Reid cleared the doorway, following the sound of a meltdown, Dawson looked up from his spot on the floor. To Reid's surprise, he didn't look angry at all. More than anything, he seemed exasperated. "Oh, good. Can you hold this spot for me while I staple?"

Reid didn't hesitate. He crossed the room, dropped to his knees, and held the canvas against the wood frame where Dawson indicated.

Dawson used a staple gun to pin it in place. "I don't have enough hands for this," Dawson muttered while moving to the next spot. "A lot of Milo's clients want weirdly shaped paintings to fit their decor, uncaring that canvas doesn't come in that shape and someone has to figure out how to make it happen."

Reid eyed the canvas. The frame was shaped like stairs and Dawson had done a pretty damn wonderful job of stretching the canvas to fit without creases. "You're doing an impressive job. I'm sure Milo really appreciates this."

Dawson grunted. "It's the least I can do, since he's the one carrying us."

Reid kept his gaze locked on their task. He didn't want to overstep immediately, especially since he needed Dawson to give him some answers, but Reid couldn't resist. "You carry each other. That's what makes the two of you such an amazing pair. You take care of each other and have each other's backs. It's beautiful to see."

Dawson didn't respond right away. When he did, his voice came out quiet. "Thanks for that. With this project fighting me, I've been feeling kind of useless today."

"With Malia in town, I know the feeling." Reid couldn't stop himself. He saw his opening and had to take it. "I keep offering to take her places while Valor works, so she's not alone all day, but he keeps turning me down. I'm pretty sure I'm failing at this boyfriend thing."

"Don't worry over it. She's not alone. Valor

always takes a week of vacation when his mom is here. Milo and I had lunch with them earlier today." Dawson glanced up smiling, oblivious to the sledgehammer he had just taken to Reid's life. "Malia was adorable. She kept doting on Milo, hugging him and threatening to put him in her suitcase and take him home. Milo needs more of that in his life."

Reid kept a smile in place that he didn't feel. Valor had been lying to him. He hadn't been working at all this week. Valor just didn't want Reid around. Reid fought to keep his voice normal and light in the face of betrayal. "Malia is sweet. I'm sure she saw a kindred spirit in Milo."

Milo appeared in the doorway. "I'd planned to bring everyone something to drink, but when I got to the kitchen, I realized I don't know what you like, Reid. We have bottled water, soda, and beer."

Reid's heart beat so fast in his chest that barely any oxygen reached his brain. He had to get out of there. Valor had been lying to him, blowing him off and keeping him away from his mom. Reid had lost his heart to a liar. He had trusted Valor. If Valor wasn't honest about this week, what else had he been lying about? Was everything a lie? He had never once questioned Valor's words. Now nothing felt real any longer.

Reid tried pulling himself together. He was an actor. Reid was used to performing under pressure. He called upon all his skills to get him through the moment. "Don't worry about me. I just wanted to stop by and see you guys. We haven't really spoken since I started dating Valor, and Christmas is right around the corner. I haven't talked things over with Valor yet, but I would love for us to get together and do something—like a family would." It wasn't complete bullshit. Reid had been thinking about that, but it wouldn't happen now and wasn't why he was here. Reid obviously meant nothing to Valor. Less than nothing, if he could keep lying to Reid nonstop.

Dawson and Milo exchanged glances—like holding a silent conversation and gauging each other's reaction. Milo smiled and Dawson looked Reid's way. "We'd like that. Valor is like family to me and we should try to start some sort of holiday tradition."

Reid nodded. The canvas was complete, so he pushed to his feet. His smile got harder to hold by the second. "Fantastic. I'll bring it up to Valor and we can start planning something." Reid had come here for different answers and gotten more than he expected. It didn't matter now what Valor's secret scandal was, because they were done. "I'll let you two get back to work."

Dawson stood and brushed off his knees. "Thank you for helping me. This might've taken me all day without the extra set of hands."

Milo huffed. "I've been offering to help all day."

With an indulgent smile, Dawson kissed the tip of Milo's nose. "I know, baby, but you do too much already. This job was on me."

For a moment, Reid couldn't move while he stared at Milo and Dawson. They were so in love and had such a beautiful dynamic. Reid had almost ruined their relationship thanks to his ugly past. It was no wonder Valor couldn't love him and didn't hesitate to tell him lies to keep Reid away from his mom. Valor treated Reid exactly as he had shown he deserved. That didn't mean Reid had to stick around for it.

"It was my pleasure." With those words hanging between them, Reid walked away. Even he heard the pain in his voice. Reid didn't look back. This was Valor's family. Reid needed to remember that and go back to his nothingness. It was for the best. If Reid had been honest with himself, even once, he should have known they never stood a chance. No doubt karma had been looking to even the score with him for years. The way the broken pieces of his heart rattled in his chest while Reid drove home said karma had found its scales. He had been an unworthy man living a life above him. That was over now. No doubt Valor had been too scared for Reid's mental health to tell him to go away. Reid should have read the signs, but he had been too busy falling in love.

He would give Valor his freedom. Reid didn't think Valor was the type of man to lie under normal circumstances. It was Reid. Valor had always considered Reid broken. It made sense he would feel stuck with Reid. Goddamn, Reid was a blind idiot. He had really thought they were going somewhere big. Reid rubbed his chest. His eyes burned, but he couldn't cry. Reid had burned through all his tears as a child. Now he was just an empty shell. Valor had seen that. He had known Reid wasn't human. They had never stood a chance.

VALOR: *Mom wants to know if you'd like to come to dinner after your rehearsal.*

VALOR: *I'm guessing you probably forgot to turn your phone back on after rehearsal last night. Will you come see Mom off at the airport with me? She wants to say goodbye. I tried calling, but it went straight to voicemail.*

VALOR: *Okay. What the hell? Are you dead or just ignoring me?*

VALOR: *I'm guessing you're ignoring me since you won't answer my calls, you've changed the code to your gate, and security wouldn't let me see you at the theater. Can you at least tell me what I've done?*

VALOR: DAWSON TELLS ME THAT YOU TWO TALKED *about doing a family thing for Christmas. I also gathered you learned I was off work the week of Mom's visit. Will you please let me explain?*

VALOR: I NEVER THOUGHT IT WOULD END LIKE *this.*

SIX

EVERY SECOND of every day that Valor spent without Reid was hell. He had done everything sane he could think to do to talk to Reid. He had called, gone by his house and work. Hell, Valor had even started getting coffee at the ridiculously overpriced coffee shop across the street from Reid's theater each morning like a proper stalker. Reid never showed. Valor never even caught a glimpse of him. Christmas came and went, forcing Valor to admit to Dawson that he had lied to Reid and ruined everything. That conversation had led to him explaining why he had done such a terrible thing. The conversation had been surprisingly easy. Valor hadn't forced his lips to shape the words in over twenty years and only then in counseling. As the story had flowed from Valor while Dawson listened without judgment, Valor had made a monumental discovery. Reid would have understood, and Valor was a coward. Unfortunately, while sitting in a booth at The Back Porch, Valor could have these thoughts all day. They meant nothing. He was too late in his guilt and self-discovery. Reid had disappeared and Valor didn't think he would ever see him again.

Reid was a celebrity. Valor couldn't rush his front door or wait by his car. He was inaccessible unless he wanted to see someone, and Reid decidedly did not want to see Valor. Valor got it. Reid had been vulnerable with him and let him in. Valor had repaid Reid's trust by treating him like he didn't want Reid around his mom, lying, and keeping secrets. Reid had every right to be done. Valor just wished he had one last chance to say all the things he hadn't gotten to say. They would still be over, and Valor's heart would still be shattered, but maybe his chest would stop feeling like an elephant had used it as a seat. He felt broken and scattered all the time now. Valor imagined he would get killed soon because his head was never in his work anymore. All he did all hours of the day was plot ways to see Reid and ache for him. Valor didn't know how to stop.

"Hi. I haven't seen you in a while."

Valor blinked at the sudden appearance of the tiny blond. Not only was he surprised to see Tobin, he couldn't believe Tobin spoke to him, considering... unless he didn't know. "Hey." Valor motioned toward the empty side of the booth across from him. "Have a seat. Are you dropping off croissants? If so, where are they? I don't want to miss out."

Tobin's green eyes flashed with humor. "I've just passed them along to Wrecker. I'm sure you won't miss out if you order now. How have you been? With Reid out of town, I rarely leave my apartment to see anyone." Tobin paused. "Is that sad? I sounded pathetic right then, didn't I?"

A genuine smile tugged at Valor's lips. He honestly liked Tobin. He was anti-social and owned it. Without Reid dragging him around, he never went anywhere. Reid being out of town explained a lot. Valor needed more info. "I'm sure Reid will be back to forcing you to go everywhere with him as soon as he gets home."

A line appeared between Tobin's eyebrows. "He got home last night."

Valor made a dismissive motion. "Sorry. I meant once he's had some time to rest. He's never really back home until he's had a few days to unpack and get settled."

Tobin's expression cleared. "That's true. I probably have at least two more days' reprieve before he's back to being a tornado." Tobin eyed him for a second. "You're not in uniform. Are you off today?"

An idea struck as Valor nodded. "Yeah. I took the day off, hoping to surprise Reid, but I forgot he changed the damn code at his gate, and I didn't write down the recent one. So I guess I'm stuck waiting until he wakes up and calls."

Tobin's expression darkened. His brow furrowed with worry. "Yeah. He's so much braver than I am. I can't imagine having to deal with everything he does. All those letters from pedophiles, wanting more details about his childhood. It's sickening. Now he has that one sending him flowers and love notes, salivating over having seen the video of him with that awful producer. It's a nightmare. I imagine he never feels safe. It's a good thing he has you or I would never sleep from worrying about him."

Valor felt sick. Reid had never said any of that to him. In fact, Reid had always pretended he had no problems while they had been dating. It stung that Reid suffered in silence. It was also terrifying how much Reid would endure alone just so he wouldn't appear less in Valor's eyes. He supposed they had that in common. "No one will hurt him on my watch." Even Valor heard the determination in his voice.

A slight smile touched Tobin's lips. "I have the new code, if you need it."

It was hard, but Valor managed to temper his reaction. "That would be great. Thank you."

Tobin waved off Valor's thanks as he dug out his phone. "It's no problem. Reid texted it to me right before he left town. He had to go pretty suddenly, which happens sometimes when he lands a big role, or another actor gets hurt on a play that's already running. They call Reid in to save the day, which you know. My point is, he didn't have time to stop by to see me before he left. So he sent me the new gate code in case I needed to crash at his place while he was gone. I don't know why he's always offering. I never accept, but he has an enormous heart. It's 4306."

Valor barely stopped himself from flying to his feet. "Thank you. I'll head that way. Don't tell him I'm coming."

Tobin flashed him a bright smile. "I won't ruin the surprise. We already have plans later this week anyhow."

Damn. Reid would tell Tobin when they got together about Valor being a liar, and Tobin would never speak to him again after today. Valor wasn't used to being the bad guy. The title chaffed. He found himself turning sincere and regretting using Tobin to get closer to Reid. "It was good to see you. Are you doing okay?"

Tobin's smile slipped away. He shrugged. Valor realized his eyes were a bit black underneath and he didn't look so great. "I'm making it." He stood, as if Valor's question made him uncomfortable. "I'll see you around."

Valor nodded, feeling like shit. He had never considered himself an awful person before meeting Reid. It was like falling in love with someone out of his league had broken him somehow.

"Take care."

Valor watched Tobin leave, taking in how slowly he moved and how tired he looked. Valor made a mental list of ways he could help while trying to give Tobin time to drive away before coming to his feet. As much as Valor wanted to rush to use the information he had tricked from Tobin, Valor wondered if he was making a mistake. It was possible Reid was better off without him. Plus, he had been working out of town and could have met someone else. Then Valor thought about the reasons Tobin had given for Reid changing his gate code, and a seething rage settled in Valor's chest. No one fucked with Reid. Maybe Valor was a complete piece of shit and didn't deserve Reid, but no one hurt Reid. Reid belonged to Valor. Valor would make things right if it was the last thing he did. If he couldn't, then Valor would still spend the rest of his days loving Reid. His heart would never belong to anyone else.

Six weeks in an extremely cold New York had done nothing to cool the sting of Reid's heartbreak. Thankfully, he had been playing the part of a mourning husband and bitter detective. Reid hadn't been forced to fake many smiles. At least he had been too busy to let the real heartache set in. Reid couldn't say the same now. His house felt empty. Since he had blocked Valor's number, his phone stayed silent. Other than health updates from Tobin, Valor hadn't heard from anyone. That pretty much summed up his life in a nutshell from the moment he had cut his mother from his life eight years ago.

Reid was tired, but he wasn't. His eyelids were heavy, but his body was restless. No matter what he tried, his mind wouldn't still. It was the quiet. He

just needed to down some coffee and then visit everyone at the playhouse. In between the big productions, there was always some minor part he could play to keep him moving. That was all Reid could do—keep heading forward. He didn't need anyone.

After throwing on a clean t-shirt, Reid checked his reflection. He looked rough. His blue eyes appeared flat—like he had died on the inside. In all honesty, Reid admitted that had happened long ago. He was just now noticing people could tell by looking at him. His hair needed a trim. He needed to shave. Reid swore he looked ten years older today. He found himself sitting on the bench at the end of his bed, staring at nothing. Reid had been working nonstop since he was ten. At twenty-six, he wondered if he was already facing his midlife crisis. Maybe he should leave L.A.

Reid's gaze moved back to his reflection. He hadn't minded the cold that much. Maybe he should look into making the move to New York permanently. His house was immense. It was too much for one person. He could get an apartment in the city and take up walking everywhere... or buy a farm in a nearby county. His life was already empty. Maybe he should embrace it somewhere else. It wasn't like L.A. had been kind to him. In fact, L.A. felt ten times colder to Reid.

A motion out the corner of his eye startled Reid. He turned his head, expecting the cleaning service that came twice a week. Instead, he found Valor. Reid couldn't move. Shock left him speechless.

Valor wore jeans and a Henley. He looked sexy as hell, if not a little nervous. "You changed your gate code but not the code to the front door."

"I never expected you to scale the fence." Even Reid couldn't believe how calm he sounded.

"I didn't." He didn't offer any further clues as to how he had gotten past the gate. Instead, Valor moved on like he hadn't broken into Reid's house. "I've been calling and texting."

"I blocked your number."

Valor dropped his chin for a moment, as if absorbing the blow. When he met Reid's stare again, he looked determined. "I didn't want you spending time alone with Mom."

Reid had figured that much out for himself, but damn. It hurt hearing Valor say the words aloud, giving them power. Reid looked away. He didn't have the energy to fight, and there was no way he could physically throw Valor out. One of those two things was about to happen, and Reid already felt exhausted from it.

"It's not because of anything you did," Valor said, moving farther into the room. "It's because she tells everything she knows, and I didn't want her to tell you about me." Valor leaned against Reid's dresser. For a long moment, they stared at each other in silence. Reid fought the urge to rub his chest, massaging away the emptiness there. Valor shifted nervously, crossing and uncrossing his arms until he ended up bracing his hands on the dresser on either side of his hips. He took an audible breath—like searching for courage. Reid's curiosity was at an all-time high. "Do you know who Wayne Rainier is?"

The sudden question had Reid blinking in confusion. "Yeah. He's that high school baseball coach who drugged and raped a bunch of kids, spanning like decades. Everyone has heard that one." As the words left his mouth, the truth dawned on Reid. Suddenly, like a light switch was thrown, everything about Valor made sense. His desire to be a cop, saving every child he could. All the community projects and refusing to go home to Hawaii. Conversations where they had clicked on every level took on a whole new light. "Holy shit." The words fell from Reid's lips, sounding breathless as the weight of what he had just learned landed.

Valor chewed his bottom lip, seemingly satisfied with Reid's conclusion and obviously not intending to say more.

Reid—on the other hand—had plenty to say. "But I don't understand. You could've said that to me. Seriously, me of all people. If there was no one else on the planet who you could've said that to, it should've been me."

Valor gave him a solemn nod. "I know, but coming to L.A. saved me, and I didn't want to lose the identity I found here. The peace."

Reid didn't think he could fault Valor for that since he had just been thinking about leaving L.A. for the same reason, but still. "We're not talking about an entire town. You made the conscious decision to lie to me and shut me out, making me feel like I wasn't good enough to be around your family. You chose your secrets over us. Telling you about Milo's mom blackmailing me and admitting what she had on me, that was one of the hardest things I've ever done in my life. I did it because I didn't want to hurt you. When it came to be your turn, you weren't willing to do the same for me."

"I'm here now. I would've been here sooner, if you would've let me."

That was true, but it felt too late for Reid's heart. "I'm moving to New York."

Valor crossed his arms and uncrossed them again, as if fighting himself. Finally, he settled down. "Why?"

"There's nothing here for me." At that moment, those words felt like the most honest thing Reid had said in years.

"I am."

"Are you, though?" As the question left his lips, Reid fully embraced how deeply Valor had cut him. He had poured the worst of himself out for Valor's perusal, and—in the end—he just hadn't been that important. "Because I have to say, it feels a hell of a lot like I've spent the last several months loving someone who cares not at all about me."

Surprise crossed Valor's features—like he hadn't expected Reid would stick up for himself. "I love you."

Despite being caught off guard by Valor's admission, Reid couldn't back down now. He hadn't forgotten this was just the lie he had caught, and he was tired of being expected to let everything go.

Reid's temper rose to the surface. He had stayed quiet his whole life, hoping the people who were supposed to love him would. Reid couldn't do it anymore. He snorted. "Everyone who says that to me always only shows me the opposite. You're not special. Please show yourself out the same way you came in."

Valor pushed away from the dresser. He dug inside his pocket and came out with a ring box. Valor set it on the dresser. "Merry Christmas."

Reid's eyes stayed glued on the box as Valor headed for the door. "What is that?"

Valor hesitated. He glanced over his shoulder. "Your Christmas gift. Since I didn't see you then, I want you to have it now, even if it means nothing to you."

With his heart in his throat, Reid stood and moved to the dresser. He flipped open the box. A gold and platinum ring with a diamond in the center stared up at him. It was unmistakably a wedding band. For a moment, he didn't move. He couldn't speak. His throat no longer worked. Reid opened one of the small drawers that lined the top half of his dresser and pulled out a similar box.

He held the box out to Valor. "Merry Christmas."

Valor didn't accept the gift right away. Like Reid,

he seemed to be fighting an inner battle. Finally, Valor reached for the box and flipped it open. He stared at the contents in silence. Reid knew what he saw—an eerily similar wedding band. Valor took an audibly shaken breath, and then another.

"Is this really what I fucked up?"

Reid couldn't answer. He didn't know how to respond. It seemed like one second they had been perfect, and then the next, everything had been gone. Reid didn't know how they had gotten here.

Valor closed the distance between them. He set his gift on the dresser and picked up the one he had given to Reid. Before Reid could beg him not to take it away, Valor dropped to one knee.

"I love you, Reid. I am in love with you. Fuck if I know how things got this screwed up, but I don't want to live without you. Will you please marry me? I will tell you anything you want to know. If you let me, I'll spend the rest of my life making this right. Trust me, I know I am as far from perfect as a man can get, but I swear no one will ever love you as much as I do. In fact, I love you so goddamn much that I couldn't endure the thought of you looking at me like I was anything less than the man you met. I panicked and fucked up, but it will never happen again."

Reid's heart had moved to his throat and wouldn't budge. He didn't know if Valor realized he was crying, but Valor wasn't making any move to hide his tears. Without thought, Reid found himself cupping Valor's face and swiping away the tears with his thumbs. If Reid knew nothing else, he knew he loved Valor and he would eventually fuck up too. He hoped—when that day came—Valor didn't make him beg the way he had.

"I love you." The words came out in a harsh whisper, proving how hard Reid had to work to speak. "You should have told me." Reid's voice got firmer by the second. "You should've said something, so I could've been prepared with a snarky-ass comment when your mom called that shit your scandal. What the fuck? How dare she?" The more Reid thought about it, the angrier he got. "No one hurts my future husband. Are you fucking kidding me? And then, after that, she tried to use me to drag you back to that place. I can't fucking believe it."

Valor pressed his lips together—like he fought back laughter. "Was that a yes?"

Heat filled Reid's cheeks as he realized how carried away he had gotten. "Yes."

Valor shot to his feet and overcame Reid. As their lips met, Reid almost fell apart. He couldn't recall the last time he'd cried, but he felt the tears press against the backs of his eyes. Reid thought they would never touch again. He thought he had lost this for good. The idea nearly took out his knees.

Before he could stop himself, Reid bit Valor's bottom lip. "Don't you ever lie to me again."

Valor rubbed his lip, but he didn't stop smiling. "Yes, sir." Valor plucked the ring from the box. "Put this on."

Reid held out his hand and let Valor slip the ring onto his finger. He swore the air thinned as he watched the gold and platinum circle slip across his skin, finding its place. His gaze met Valor's. "It fits."

Valor looked smug. "One of the many nonsensical conversations we've had in our quest to know everything about each other. It looks perfect on you."

Reid's throat swelled again, making his voice come out in a whisper. "I've missed you. So much."

Valor grabbed two handfuls of Reid's ass and lifted, leaving Reid no other choice but to cling to Valor's shoulders and wrap his legs around Valor's waist. His heated expression had Reid's mouth going dry. "Every day has been hell without you." Valor sounded hoarse. His serious and hurt tone squeezed

Reid's heart in his chest. "Please don't ever ignore me like that again."

"Don't ever lie to me again."

Valor gave him a sharp nod. "Deal."

Reid stared down into the face of the man he loved and knew everything would be okay. He was still angry and hurt, but those feelings had shifted to a new target. Considering how shitty his mother was, it was easy for Reid to transfer his rage to Valor's mom. He knew Valor still wasn't innocent. Valor had still chosen to lie, but it was a lie Reid understood. If he could hide his past, he would. Hell, he had done some horrible things to keep it hidden. Reid couldn't fault Valor for doing what he needed to do to survive and stay sane. In fact, Reid's love for him grew. Surviving was a hell of a lot harder than people knew.

He swiped his lips across Reid's. "I love you." Reid lightly sucked Valor's bottom lip. "I love you so much."

Valor headed for the bed. "I love you too." He set Reid on the edge of the bed. "I really need to hold you for a little while, if you're not busy."

A smile tugged at Reid's lips. "I've got time, but you should probably strip. You know, for comfort's sake."

Valor nodded, looking solemn. "Yeah. Probably. Wearing jeans and whatnot to bed is pretty uncomfortable. You should do the same."

It was hard, but Reid managed to keep his expression serious. "True. You know me, I'm usually nude when I go to bed."

"We shouldn't fuck with tradition."

They stared at each other for a single heartbeat, before flying into action. Clothes flew in every direction. A chuckle rose in Reid's throat at their desperation to be naked together. The sound died on a moan as Valor's mouth covered his. Their tongues met and stroked. Reid's hands smoothed up Valor's chest before meeting behind his neck. As Valor crawled onto the bed and covered Reid's body with his, Reid felt the weeks they had been apart disappearing. This had always been his soulmate. He wouldn't forget again.

THE MIXTURE OF LOVE, RELIEF, HAPPINESS, AND leftover misery racing through Valor's veins made him unstable. He wanted to shout at the top of his lungs in celebration. Reid had agreed to marry him, making him the happiest man alive. But Valor's insides still shook from the aftermath of being without Reid, and that horrible feeling wouldn't go away until he reclaimed Reid in every way. Reid being nude beneath him was an excellent start. He couldn't stop kissing Reid, hoping to assuage his heart.

A thought hit Valor. Panic had him needing to clear up one more detail right away. He pulled away and brushed Reid's hair away from his face so he could hold his stare.

"If you still want to move to New York, you know I'll follow you anywhere."

Reid shook his head. "I was having a moment, but I'm not a runner. Not really. You're all I need."

Valor buried his face in the crook of Reid's neck and inhaled. In the weeks he had been without Reid, Valor had made a lot of recent discoveries about himself through self-reflection. Before Reid, Valor had been certain he was healed. He thought all the community work and helping teenagers had made him whole, but he hadn't stopped to look at his personal life. Valor had been nothing but one-night stands and no commitment his entire adult life. While he had accepted that he likely wasn't capable of romantic love, deep down, he had known the truth. Valor had been scared to let anyone too close until he met someone just like him. He hadn't wanted to be exposed and vulnerable. Valor needed to be seen as strong after being helpless. Losing Reid had shown him the truth. Valor wasn't strong at all. Reid was the strong one.

"Valor?"

"Yes, baby?"

Reid's arms tightened around him. "Are you okay?"

Valor nodded.

Reid kissed his temple. "Do you plan to make love to me?"

Valor nodded.

He felt Reid smile against his skin. "Sometime today?"

Valor nodded.

Reid ran his fingertips up and down Valor's spine. "There's no rush. You're always safe with me. I'll take care of you."

Valor believed. Reid was an amazing person. He deserved a beautiful life filled with love, affection, touches, and kisses. Valor would start today. His lips brushed Reid's neck. Once there, Valor's hunger stirred. He needed more. He opened his mouth over the side of Reid's neck. It hit him. Valor was starved but not for sex. He needed this. Valor craved holding

Reid and kissing him. He needed to feel close and intimate. Sex had absolutely nothing to do with it at the moment. He needed to feel connected. Inseparable.

Reid grabbed a handful of blanket and tugged before tossing it over them. "Stay put, gorgeous. I'll hold you."

The backs of Valor's eyes burned. Never before had he felt more understood than he had since meeting Reid. It was like—without ever saying the words—they had known they were exactly what the other needed. Inside, where no one else could see, they were exactly alike. Two halves of the same whole. They had the rest of their lives to make love. Right now, they were healing each other with affection.

Reid's lips skimmed Valor's shoulder. "This is perfect."

It really was. Valor couldn't wait to spend the rest of his life right here.

THE DAY PASSED IN A BLUR. THEY NEVER DRESSED or left the bed. Instead, they talked nonstop while stealing kisses and playing footsie beneath the covers. Reid told him about his six weeks in New York while Valor talked about growing up in Hawaii. The town he had lived in had been large but still intolerant. Luckily, Valor had been good at sports, giving him something to keep him busy until moving to California. The way his face lit when he talked about caring for Dawson and Sergio warmed Reid's heart. He was proud to have fallen in love with such a good man.

"I stopped by the gallery to see Dawson and Milo before I left town."

Valor nodded. "Dawson told me."

"They're adorably happy together."

Valor eyed him for a moment, as if trying to decipher where Reid was headed with this. "They're meant to be, I guess."

"I feel guilty all the time," Reid admitted. Anytime he thought about Milo and Dawson, he hated the way he felt.

"You have no reason to feel guilty. They're fine. To be honest, I'm pretty sure they're completely unbreakable."

Reid shrugged, feeling exposed. "I know, but still." Reid took a breath and dove in, trying to explain. "For a lot of years, I immersed myself in my role of being the famous actor. I hid behind the mask of someone who earned it."

"You did earn it."

Reid waved away Valor's argument. "Just listen."

Valor made a show of pressing his lips together.

As serious as their conversation was, Reid couldn't help but smile at Valor's antics. Reid shook his head and kept going. "What I'm trying to say is that I hid behind a mask of fame. I pulled all my confidence from pretending to be exactly what everyone expected. Arrogant and bored. Now I don't have that anymore, so I don't know how to behave around anyone anymore. With Dawson, Milo, and your mom, I feel like I need them to like me or maybe you'll stop loving me, but I don't have a mask to hide behind. It's just me and just me isn't good enough for any of them."

A deep line appeared between Valor's eyebrows. "No one could make me stop loving you. But if you need reassurance, my mom really does love you after only one meeting. It was all me, keeping you away from her. She doesn't know how to deal with what happened to me, so it's easier for her to think of it as dirty laundry. That way, she doesn't feel like she was wrong to trust me spending so much time with a grown stranger. Now that I'm grown, she minimizes everything like it's just people gossiping, and I can't stomach it. That's not on you. I need you to understand that, because avoiding my parents and their way of handling my pain, that's how I've survived."

Reid didn't hesitate to have Valor's back. "I can do that. Whatever you need to get through this life, I'm with you."

A slight smile touched Valor's lips. He toyed with Reid's fingers. "As to Milo and Dawson, you're not to blame for how far Milo's mom would go to keep him where she wants him. Rachel has never seen Milo as anything other than a way to make herself look good. She did artificial insemination so she wouldn't have any nasty second parent to deal with. Then she neglected Milo into being the perfect son while hiring tutors to make him as accomplished as possible. His every achievement was hers, in her eyes. She needed him to stay perfect, even if he never spoke to her. Maybe she even liked it better if he didn't talk to her. Either way, you're not responsible for how far she would go. The craziest part about the entire thing is that I'm not sure she really believed she had done anything illegal. Not when she bought that video of you or even when she blackmailed you. I truly think she only saw those things as ways to control her son. She didn't see you as a living, breathing human any more than she sees Milo as an actual person. But Milo sees you as real, and he has more heart than anyone I've ever met. He doesn't blame you for her sins."

Reid's throat swelled. He held on to every word Valor spoke.

Valor kept going, saving him. "Actually, I'm pretty sure Milo is one hundred and ten percent heart and nothing else. Every single thing he does, be it paintings, poetry, or loving Dawson, all comes from deep inside his soul. Every person who makes it inside his walls gets the same treatment. From the way he talked about you making the effort to see him, I think you scaled his walls. You don't have to worry about him hating you, and as long as he's on your side, Dawson will follow. But having said all that." Valor slid closer until he had Reid on his back, and then he straddled Reid's body. He stared down at Reid with an intensity that stole Reid's breath. "No matter how anyone else feels about you, I love you. Spending the last six weeks without you, I've come to realize that my feelings can't be shaken. Even if you hated me or never spoke to me again, I would still be drowning in love for you. You're who I want. I can't be moved."

Happiness had all Reid's worries falling away. His hands found Valor's ass. He squeezed. "You say that now, but you haven't lived under the same roof with me yet. I might drive you nuts."

He felt Valor's cock stirring between them. "Driving me to nut, is that what you said?"

A bark of laughter burst from Reid. "I think you're hearing what you want to hear."

Valor shook his head. His exaggerated innocence had Reid shaking with laughter. "No. I may be old, but I definitely heard you talking about nuts."

Reid pretended to try to get away. "Ugh. You're trying to turn things around."

Valor's innocent expression deepened as his eyes widened and he slowly blinked. "You want me to turn you around? I mean, I kind of like staring in your eyes when I nut but okay." He used his strength against Reid and flipped him onto his stomach. Valor immediately straddled Reid's body again, keeping him pinned to the bed. Reid couldn't stop laughing. Valor was too ridiculous.

"How did I fall in love with someone so weird?"

A sexy chuckle rumbled against Reid's ear as Valor kissed its shell. Reid went hard. Valor's tongue traced the outline of Reid's ear. "You're just lucky like that, I guess."

Reid had already forgotten what they were talking about. His hips left the bed as he moved against the mattress, seeking relief while also trying his damnedest to tease Valor.

"I've been so empty without you." Even Reid heard the deprivation in his voice.

"I've got what you need."

Reid knew he did. That was why he felt so needy. Valor's weight lifted from Reid's body and a whimper slipped past his lips at the loss. Before he could beg Valor to come back, slippery fingers probed his crack and asshole. A moan stuck in Reid's throat.

"Damn, your body is so beautiful. It almost matches your gorgeous heart."

The way Reid moved restlessly beneath Valor's touch was out of his control. Another whimper escaped when he heard the crinkle of the condom wrapper. It was almost time. A pant burst from him. His entire body tensed in anticipation. Valor's teeth sank into Reid's ass cheek. Reid saw stars. He hadn't been this turned on in a while. Every brush against his skin brought him closer to the edge. Valor dragged Reid's hips back until Reid was on his knees. Reid cried out as Valor pushed his way inside. All Reid could do was hold on while Valor pounded inside him. He no longer cared about anything but the pleasure. Reid needed release. He begged for it. Even though he couldn't understand his own words, Valor knew what Reid craved. Valor changed angles and sent Reid soaring. He stopped breathing. His entire body shook with ecstasy. Every sense he possessed dampened, even as the world exploded around him with color and light. Reid cried Valor's name as Valor bit his shoulder, muffling his own screams.

As they collapsed into a heap of sweaty limbs and heavy breathing, Reid prayed they were never dumb again. Even though he knew he could survive without Valor, Reid knew surviving was all it would be. Life was cold without Valor's warmth. Reid had found his home. He wouldn't lose it again.

SEVEN

THE MURMUR OF INAUDIBLE VOICES, laughter, and glasses clinking filled the air. Tobin sat in the corner, trying to make himself smaller. Reid had such a beautiful home. Tonight, it was filled with equally beautiful people. Everyone from the playhouse was there. Tobin knew everyone by name and face, even though Reid was the only one who ever spoke to him. That was typical Reid, though. No one was below or above him. To all the other actors, Tobin was invisible. He was the guy who brought in food to the green room while they worked. Tobin was no one to them. In fact, besides Reid, Tobin doubted any one of them knew he existed. Tobin kind of liked it that way. He was uncomfortable around strangers.

Reid and Valor's engagement party took place around Tobin. He was never really a part of anything. Tobin was the guy on the fringes of everything, wishing he could go home. It had been that way his entire life. Tobin didn't know what to say to people he didn't know. He enjoyed the quiet and baking. Neither of those things made for stimulating conversation.

A nervous flutter stirred in Tobin's gut for no reason. As he pressed his hand against his stomach, Tobin saw him. His jet-black hair caught the light, fascinating Tobin. Sergio hugged Valor. His smile was so infectious, Tobin smiled in response. Tobin forced the grin from his face when he realized what he had done. He couldn't help himself. Sergio was all gleaming white teeth and deep lines around his mouth. Tobin swore he could see the naughty twinkle in Sergio's eyes from across the room. His body was sleek, and his dark tan skin made his smile seem even brighter. The man was ridiculously gorgeous. That one flirtatious meeting between them still made Tobin's cheeks burn. The way Sergio had looked at him the day they met had kept Tobin warm much longer than he cared to admit.

Sergio's head turned from side to side as he visibly scanned the room. His gaze landed on Tobin and didn't move. Tobin tried again to make himself smaller. It was too late. Sergio's smile turned wicked as he headed Tobin's way. He swore even the way Sergio carried himself changed the moment he spotted Tobin. Tobin's heart sped. He didn't doubt for a second that Sergio would be shameless in bed. As Tobin watched Sergio head his way, the truth sideswiped Tobin in a way he never expected. He didn't want to die. Tobin had so much left to experience. There was so much he still wanted to do. He hadn't scratched a single item from his bucket list. Maybe Sergio would be the first.

A RANGE OF EMOTIONS STIRRED IN VALOR'S chest as his engagement party happened around him. Above all else, he was over the moon to be marrying Reid. Underneath that happiness, Valor had a lot of other stuff going on too. First, Milo and Dawson were there. Not only were they there, they had seemed genuinely thrilled to be invited and happy to see Reid. That mattered. In his heart, Dawson would always be Valor's son and Milo his son-in-law. He wanted them to be a family, getting together on holidays and whatnot. Valor loved that they were getting along. He could see a future where they got to be a proper family, finally. It was a dynamic they all needed. Maybe, one day, Sergio would join the fray.

Secondly, and less thrilling, his parents were not there. While his mom had claimed—once again—that his dad was too poorly to travel, Valor knew that was bullshit. His dad was in perfect health. Valor rubbed his chest. He knew the truth. His dad still believed Valor's "little scandal" had turned him gay. If he had ever bothered to take notice, his dad would have seen Valor had been born this way. Valor wanted to claim it didn't matter they weren't there, but it did. However, Valor would be damned if anyone saw him bleed over it. At the end of the day, Reid would still be marrying him soon and nothing mattered more than that. They would enjoy the family they chose together.

Speaking of their chosen family, Valor couldn't tear his eyes away from Sergio and Tobin. Tobin was like a brother to Reid, and Valor cared what happened to him. Under normal circumstances, and despite also loving Sergio like a son, Valor would have been concerned about Sergio hurting Tobin. It wasn't that Sergio was the love them and then leave them type. Sergio's heart had been broken recently.

Valor didn't want Tobin to become the rebound guy, but that wasn't what he saw now. They were visibly more animated in each other's company. Valor was fascinated.

Reid's arms encircled Valor's waist from behind. He pressed his lips to Valor's shoulder. "What's up, sexy? Are you tired already?"

A hum rose in Valor's throat. He never got tired of Reid's touch. As much as he wanted to be alone with Reid, he knew he needed to focus on something else. Valor nodded toward where Tobin and Sergio sat laughing and talking. "It looks like Sergio and Tobin have hit it off."

Reid held on tighter. "That's good. Tobin needs all the friends he can get."

A snort escaped Valor. "I don't think Sergio has friendship in mind."

He felt Reid shrug. "That's fine. Tobin needs some of that too."

Valor turned in Reid's arms and hauled Reid against him. "I need some of that myself."

The bright smile Reid wore, and the way he rolled his eyes at Valor's ridiculousness, was what made Valor's life worth living. "We can't sneak away from our engagement party." His expression shifted. For a moment, Reid looked thoughtful. "I do need to show you something, though." His gaze skimmed the room before landing on Milo. He linked fingers with Valor and headed that way. The moment he reached where Dawson and Milo sat huddled together, Reid bent and touched his lips to Milo's ear, keeping their conversation private.

Milo's expression gave nothing away as he nodded before saying something quietly back to Reid.

With no relief to his curiosity, Reid headed down the hall. He spoke over his shoulder as they went. "Milo will cover for us for a minute. I have a surprise for you."

Since they had gotten engaged three months earlier, they had barely spent a moment out of each other's sight. Unless they were working, they were together. Valor had moved in with Reid the weekend after they had decided to marry. Since they were always together, Valor couldn't imagine Reid sneaking in a surprise for him, but he smiled at the idea. As they reached their bedroom, a smile that felt wicked even to him pulled at Valor's lips. He liked where this was headed. Unfortunately, Reid bypassed their bed and kept going, headed for his private sitting room through a door next to their bathroom. Valor rarely stepped foot inside the room because it was where Reid rehearsed his lines. As much as Valor loved watching Reid work, he knew Reid needed peace to perfect his roles.

Reid flipped on the lights as they came through the door. "Do you remember the day we met?"

As if Valor could forget. "Of course." They had met at Milo's gallery.

"You know how I bought that painting of Dawson?"

Valor tried not to think of that. Since Dawson was like a son to Valor, he couldn't even bring himself to look at the erotic image Reid had purchased. Plus, he kind of hated the idea that Reid would look at Dawson in a sexual light. Jealousy was rarely reasonable. The only saving grace from Reid buying Dawson's image was that he had also commissioned a private piece in Valor's image. That was another reason Valor never visited Reid's sitting room. Both paintings hung in this room. Valor couldn't bring himself to look at either. While Milo had created Valor's painting from a selfie Valor took, Valor still blushed each time he thought about doing such a thing. All Milo's paintings were erotic. Valor felt like an idiot, even though he had made ten grand from that photo. He forced himself to move past his embarrassment.

"How could I forget? I'm uncomfortable thinking about it."

Reid nodded, looking understanding. "Yeah, I figured you probably wouldn't want an erotic image of someone you think of like a son hanging in your house. Plus, it turns out that Milo hadn't really wanted to sell that painting. Not to mention the whole 'I tried to ruin their marriage thing.' So we came to terms and made a trade."

Valor had to force his brain to move past Reid calling this place his house. While Valor lived here, this gigantic place was Reid's home. Reid was the one who had worked for everything Valor now enjoyed. That part still felt weird, but Valor knew he needed to get over it. His gaze automatically moved to where Dawson's painting had been. A new image hung in its place. Valor's breath caught. It was them. Reid and Valor were in bed. Valor's eyes were closed, and Reid's lips were pressed to his chest. Without thought, Valor moved closer to the canvas. He swore the image radiated love.

"How?" It was the only word he could form.

Reid moved to his side and linked fingers with Valor. "I took the picture while you were sleeping and sent it to Milo. He gave it life, of course. You know how he does. He can bring beauty to life like no one I've ever seen."

Valor had to force himself not to touch the painting. His eyes watered from not wanting to blink. "It's perfect."

"I'm glad you like it."

There was something about Reid's tone. Valor immediately sought his gaze. Reid looked as solemn as his voice. "What's wrong?"

Reid squeezed Valor's hand and rubbed the back of it with his other hand. His gaze moved away. He shrugged. "I don't know. I just want you to feel like this is our home and not just some place you're invading. You've been here three months now and you still knock on doors before you enter any room I'm in—like you're a guest. It's starting to make me feel like you plan to leave one day. Marriage is supposed to be forever." His gaze found Valor's again. Reid looked sad but determined. "If you've changed your mind about wanting to marry me, I can accept that. I want you to be happy. If the past three months has started to make you feel trapped or like you were happier when we went home to our separate beds, you can say that to me."

Until that moment, Valor hadn't realized how much his discomfort with accepting Reid's wealth was affecting Reid. Valor tugged Reid into his arms and pressed his lips to Reid's forehead. "Don't say that again. You're all I want. If I could get away with marrying you tonight, I would. I don't need all the pomp and circumstance, except I want it because you deserve it." Valor leaned away and held Reid's stare. "I love you. You deserve to have the world set at your feet. That's my only regret. I don't have your money, so I can't give you anything but me. That doesn't feel like enough in the face of how much I love you, but that doesn't mean I'm giving up. The thought of getting married to you fills me with so much pride, I think I'll explode from it some days. You're not getting rid of me. Sorry if that was your plan."

Reid lightly punched him in the gut. "Ass. You know I love you and want to get married. I was just giving you one last out."

Valor shook his head and rubbed the spot where Reid hit him. "You can keep that free pass. I don't want it. You're mine and I'm yours, baby. Forever."

A radiant smile lit Reid's face. After a heartbeat, it turned wicked. "I just realized something."

Valor had to know. "What?"

Reid crowded Valor's space. "We ended up sneaking away, after all."

Valor glanced around in an exaggerated motion, making a show of being surprised. "Wow. You're so sneaky and I'm so easy. All you had to do was promise me a surprise and I was in." He rearranged his features, becoming comically serious. "All you had to do was say you wanted me to touch your dick and I would have done so."

Reid rolled his eyes and halfheartedly tried pulling away. "Okay. Whatever."

"No, no, now," Valor said, rubbing against Reid like a cat. "I can't let my fiancé feel neglected. It's my job to make sure you're ecstatic at all times. How could I live with myself if I let you go back to that party knowing I had failed you? How could I let people celebrate us and still look at myself in the mirror?"

"You're ridiculous."

Valor pretended to think it over before shrugging. "Don't care." He snagged Reid and tossed him over his shoulder. Peals of laughter sounded from Reid as Valor turned from side to side, keeping his movements as over the top as possible. "Now, where should I hide you? It has to be someplace where two people can fit comfortably but also somewhere no one will look." Valor hopped in place, making Reid's laughter grow. "I know." He took off running. There were two closets in their bedroom. Reid's, which was filled to nearly overflowing with clothes, and Valor's. It had next to nothing inside. Valor carried Reid inside and shut the door behind them. It was so dark, Valor swore his senses heightened. Reid stroked his ass. Valor let Reid slide down his body until Reid's feet touched the floor. He didn't loosen his grip. "I'm so in love with you," Valor whispered as he lowered his head.

Reid met him halfway. Their tongues stroked. Valor's pants loosened. Honestly, he had only been playing about his reasons for shutting them in the closet. It seemed Reid had other ideas. Valor had no complaints. "We have to be quick," Reid said, pulling away and going to work on Valor's clothing. It only took them a second to realize it would be faster if they stripped themselves. In a matter of moments, they were pants-less. Reid took Valor to the floor and straddled him. He nipped and licked at Valor's lips while he moved against Valor. Their cocks were trapped between them, rubbing and massaging each other. It never took much for Reid to have Valor on the edge of orgasm. No one had ever gotten through the armor encasing his heart before Reid, and it seemed that was the route to setting his body ablaze. When he had set out to rescue Reid, Valor never expected he would be the one getting saved. He would do a thousand walks of shame into parties at Reid's side to hang on to this life. Reid was worth it. Their future looked damn beautiful.

Keep an eye out for the next Candied Crush, *Beautifully Backed.*

Please consider leaving a review at the retailer where you purchased this book. Reviews really help with a book's visibility, which allows me to continue writing more stories. Thank you, Charity.

ABOUT THE AUTHOR

Charity Parkerson is an award-winning and multi-published author with several companies. Born with no filter from her brain to her mouth, she decided to take this odd quirk and insert it in her characters.

*Eight-time Readers' Favorite Award Winner
    *2015 Passionate Plume Award Finalist
    *2013 Reviewers' Choice Award Winner
    *2012 ARRA Finalist for Favorite Paranormal Romance
    *Five-time winner of The Mistress of the Darkpath

Connect with her online:

—Sign up for my newsletter: http://bit.ly/CharityNews
    —Join my readers' group on Facebook: http://bit.ly/CharitysTribe
    —Website: charityparkerson.com

—Facebook:
facebook.com/authorCharityParkerson
    facebook.com/TheMenofSin
    —Twitter: twitter.com/CharityParkerso
    —Instagram: Instagram.com/sinnerauthor

www.ingramcontent.com/pod-product-compliance
Lightning Source LLC
Chambersburg PA
CBHW061250170626
46809CB00007B/2935